"Stop."

Gwen sat up and frowned. "What do you mean, stop?"

"Stop using this pregnancy as an excuse to push people away," Alex said. "It won't work on me."

Gwen swallowed hard, her dark eyes widening slightly as she searched for meaning in his face. "I don't know what you're—"

"You want me," he interrupted. "And I want you just as badly as I did all those months ago. There's nothing wrong with that. There's no reason to try to defuse the attraction between us just because of some artificial barrier you've put in place. If you want me, give in to your feelings."

She opened her mouth to argue but his words seemed to have struck her temporarily mute. Alex thought this might be his opportunity to finally kiss her again the way he ached to....

Dear Reader,

When I was writing the end of my first book—
What Lies Beneath—something unexpected happened.
The best man and the maid of honor at the wedding
started making eyes at one another! Up until that moment,
I hadn't even considered that scenario, but once they hit
the dance floor at the reception, it became obvious to me
that my next book would have to be about Gwen and
Alex.

That's where the fun started. As an author, it is my job
to make sure my characters find their "Happily Ever
After," but also to make them earn it. I'll admit I get a
bit of sick pleasure from making their lives difficult. And
messing with Alex was even more enjoyable than usual.
What better way to make a notorious playboy quake in
his Armani loafers than to confront him with his greatest
fear—a pregnant ex-lover.

I can't wait for you to read Gwen and Alex's story.
If you enjoy it, tell me by visiting my website at
www.andrealaurence.com, like my fan page on Facebook
or follow me on Twitter. I love to hear from my readers!

Enjoy!

Andrea

ANDREA LAURENCE

MORE THAN HE EXPECTED

HARLEQUIN®

entertain, enrich, inspire™

Recycling programs
for this product may
not exist in your area.

ISBN-13: 978-0-373-73185-5

MORE THAN HE EXPECTED

www.Harlequin.com

Printed in U.S.A.

Books by Andrea Laurence

Harlequin Desire

What Lies Beneath #2152
More Than He Expected #2172

ANDREA LAURENCE

has been a lover of reading and writing stories since she learned her ABCs. She always dreamed of seeing her work in print and is thrilled to finally be able to share her books with the world. A dedicated West Coast girl transplanted to the deep South, she's working on her own "happily ever after" with her boyfriend and their collection of animals that shed like nobody's business. You can contact Andrea at her website, www.andrealaurence.com.

To Mavens Linda Howard and Linda Winstead Jones—

You are more than mentors. More than friends.
You believe in me, push me and give invaluable advice
for both career and life. I only hope that one day
I can be as generous of knowledge and spirit as you are.

And to Maven Beverly Barton —

I miss your laugh. I wish I could've shared this
experience with you, but I like to think that wherever
you are…you're proud of what I've accomplished.

Prologue

Saturday, October 20
The Wedding Reception of Will and Adrienne Taylor

It was terribly cliché for the best man to seduce the maid of honor, but damn, that was one sexy woman.

Alex had no intention of using his best friend's wedding as an opportunity to pick up women. Usually, weddings were filled with misty-eyed romantics wanting more than Alex was willing to offer. He'd planned only to wear the tux and wave goodbye as another of his friends crossed over to the dark side.

But Gwen Wright had thrown a petite, slinky wrench into his plans the minute she had strolled into the welcome breakfast. She'd been wearing a tight brown skirt and beige blouse that made her dark brown eyes pop against peaches-and-cream skin. She'd cast a quick glance at him that morning, appraising him with a small smile curving her peach lips. When their eyes met, the light of mischievousness there had intrigued him.

Will had introduced them a few minutes later, and Alex was pleased to discover she was the maid of honor and his partner in crime for the big day. He'd politely taken her hand, marveling at how soft her skin felt against his. He'd wanted to spend more time talking to her, but he didn't get the chance. She was swept into the wedding chaos and the moment passed.

He hadn't had another chance to really talk to her, much less touch her, but the anticipation was building with each hour that ticked by. He tried to focus on Will and what his job as best man entailed, since that evening had been dedicated to bachelor activities with the guys.

But tonight was a different matter. When he'd stood at the rose-covered archway beside Will and watched Gwen come toward him in that clingy pink gown, he thought he might not be able to wait much longer. As he'd escorted her down the aisle at the end of the ceremony, he'd pulled her aside and whispered, "Later," into her ear. The blush of her cheeks let him know the brief message had come across loud and clear.

And later it would be. Later than he'd planned, actually. Gwen was running the show like a seasoned professional. The first opportunity he had to talk to her was during their obligatory dance, but despite holding her in his arms, he could tell she was a million miles away—making lists, planning the cake cutting… She was a woman on a mission, and he hadn't made an inch of real progress in his pursuit of her.

Now the bride and groom had departed and the crowd had started to thin. They were quickly closing in on a "now or never" moment. From the other side of the room, he watched her direct the few men charged with taking the wedding gifts back to the apartment. Every gesture, every smile intrigued him. Alex wished he could figure out what it was about Gwen that drew him to her. The impact of her presence had been direct and immediate. If she had some kind of sexual kryptonite that weakened him, he wanted to know it.

And there must be. She'd had his undivided attention for a good part of the last thirty-six hours, and she didn't even know it. There was no argument that she was beautiful. He loved the way her curly ash-blond hair framed her heart-shaped face and the dark eyes that watched him beneath full lashes. Her petite frame was highlighted by her bridesmaid gown, showing off those shapely calves.

But there was something else about her. Something that drew him in and wouldn't let him look away. And he was determined to find out what it was.

"It's later." Gwen had been sitting for less than forty-five seconds when she heard a man's voice over her shoulder. Forty-five seconds were not nearly enough to make up for the hours she'd spent on her feet.

She was the maid of honor. It was her job to scurry about and ensure everything was on track. But she was tired. Dog tired. Regardless of what the man wanted from her, he could forget it. Even dancing with Prince Harry had less appeal than kicking off her shoes and face-planting in her bed right now.

Then she looked up and found herself smack-dab in the laser sights of none other than the best man, Alex Stanton. He was looking extraordinarily handsome tonight in his Armani tuxedo, his golden hair tamed for the special occasion. The hazel-eyed bachelor had been charming and friendly toward her for the last few days, but like Gwen, he'd been busy with wedding responsibilities of his own.

She'd tried to ignore the tingle of electricity she'd felt dance across her skin when he'd taken her arm to walk down the aisle. But then, in a brief moment alone, he'd leaned close to her ear and whispered the word "later." The single utterance was laced with such heavy meaning that it was hard to breathe for a moment. How he'd managed to roll *"I want you," "I'm going to rock your world tonight,"* and *"I hope you're prepared"* into a single word, she'd never know. He'd followed the promise with a sly smile and wink before he'd pulled away and embraced the newlyweds.

"Miss Wright, may I have this dance?"

Gwen wasn't sure if she had the strength to make it through another dance with Alex. During their first turn on the dance floor, the electric feeling had intensified; this pull that urged her to press inappropriately close to him while they swayed. She'd spent the song thinking of cheesy knock-knock jokes to distract herself. She didn't want Alex to think she was throwing herself at him. Regardless of what she'd read into his words earlier, he was dancing with her because he had to. You dance with your cousin if that's who you're paired up with in the wedding party.

But several times over the last few hours, she had felt the prickle of awareness on the nape of her neck and caught Alex watching her from across the room. There was an unabashed appreciation in his eyes as he had looked her over, making a warm flush rise to her cheeks. But instead of approaching her, he would flash his trademark smile and disappear into the crowd like a circling shark.

The reception was virtually over now. She had pretty

much given up on anything but a quiet cab ride back to her apartment, since by her estimation, "later" had come and gone a long time ago.

And yet here he was asking her to dance. His heated glance sent a shiver down her spine, a tingle of excitement overriding the pain in her toes and sending her heart racing.

Most men did not jump-start a reaction in her like this, but Alex was not most men. To say the millionaire real estate developer was out of her league was an understatement. But he didn't seem to notice.

As he held his hand out to her, there was no denying what he was offering. He wanted to fulfill his earlier promise and then some. Alex was interested in more than a dance, and by taking his hand, she was agreeing to it all. The building ache of need low in her belly and the suddenly tight press of her breasts against the confines of her fitted gown told her she was anxious to accept his offer.

Gwen looked up at her suitor. He was handsome, charming, rich…. When would she ever have another opportunity like this? She'd had her share of lovers over the years, but few could hold a candle to Alex. His reputation set tongues wagging, and she'd be lying if she'd said she didn't want some firsthand experience. She deserved a night of fun with a man who knew how to have a good time. She'd been working so hard at the hospital and helping Adrienne. Next year would be just as hectic and, if all went as planned, quite lonely. A no-strings liaison with the playboy might be just what she needed.

One last drink before rehab, so to speak.

Her eyes locked on his, her answer clear as she reached out to offer him her hand. With a triumphant smile, he eased her from her seat and swung her gently around to face him on the seamless, white dance floor.

Without hesitation, Alex wrapped his arm around Gwen's waist and pressed her tight against him. His bare palm splayed across her lower back, the heat of his touch only intensifying the pulsating desire stirring just under the surface.

She was surprised by her sudden, physical reaction to his touch. It was like a floodgate had opened. She had to suck in a ragged breath to cover the shudder that accompanied the rush of adrenaline through her veins. The spicy scent of Alex's cologne swirled in her head, mixing with the soft fragrance of roses and candle wax and making her almost light-headed. Gwen could only cling to his shoulders as they rocked back and forth to the slow, seductive music.

They stilled on the floor as the music continued but didn't pull away from one another. Instead, Alex leaned down and kissed her. It started off soft but quickly intensified once he got a taste—his tongue invading her, his mouth and hands demanding more. And she gave it to him. Gwen arched her back to press her soft body against his hard contours. He growled low in his throat, the vibration rumbling through his chest and teasing the firm peaks of her aching nipples.

Finally, the last few notes of music silenced, breaking the seductive spell that cocooned them from the surrounding world. But Alex didn't let go, as she had expected. He looked down at her, the gold flecks in his eyes almost glittering with arousal. His jaw was tense, his shoulders rising and falling with his own rapid breathing.

It was time to leave. The *how*s and *where*s and *what*s were still up in the air, but they couldn't stay on the dance floor forever. "I need to get my things out of the bridal room," she said, her voice breathy.

Alex nodded, releasing her from his embrace, and Gwen headed toward the dark hallway at the back of the boathouse.

"Keep it together, girl," she whispered to herself as she turned the knob and entered the small space. Set up for brides, the room had a vanity and mirror, a chaise lounge, a wardrobe for hanging clothes and its own bathroom. They had cleared out all of Adrienne's things earlier, but Gwen still had a few items scattered around.

She quickly checked her hair and makeup in the mirror. Her hands trembled as she grabbed her compact and mascara, stuffing them into her purse. She wasn't sure if it was nerves or arousal rattling her composure.

Gwen was reaching for her hairbrush when she heard the soft click of the door closing, then locking, behind her. She didn't turn. She only needed to look up to see Alex's reflection in the vanity's mirror, his back pressed against the door as he watched her with passion blazing in his eyes.

The *where* had apparently been decided. And she was glad.

One

Eight Months Later

"I'm almost there," Alex said. "Fashionably late, as always."

The voice of his best friend, Will Taylor, sounded through the Bluetooth-enabled sound system of his Corvette. "I'm not really worried. Just wanted to make sure you remembered how to get here."

"I'm making the last turn now," Alex lied. He was at least another fifteen minutes from the house in Sag Harbor, but it would soothe his friend's concerns. This was supposed to be a vacation. The Fourth of July was one of those laid-back holidays with no obligations. There were no schedules, so he couldn't possibly be late. "Is everyone else already there?" he asked.

"Yes."

Alex hesitated before asking one last question. "Did

Gwen end up bringing someone with her?" It was a dangerous question to ask, but he had to know. He'd re-arranged his entire schedule to come out here because she would be there.

"No, she came alone. She rode up with us this morning."

Excellent, Alex thought, although he didn't speak the word aloud. As far as he could tell, no one, including Will and Adrienne, knew about what had happened between him and Gwen last fall. So of course they wouldn't understand his interest in seeing her again. Or his burning desire to have her in his bed every night for the next five days of this trip.

"So what does that make? Ten of us?" Alex tried not to sound like he was fishing. "That's a nice, round number. I'm glad she was able to take the time off. I haven't seen her since the wedding, but I figured Adrienne would have her up for the holiday."

Will made a thoughtful sound but didn't elaborate. "We'll see you shortly then."

"Bye," Alex said, pressing the button on his steering wheel to terminate the call. Easing back into the soft leather seat, he gripped the wheel tightly and pressed his foot down on the pedal to accelerate.

Gwen would be with them in the Hamptons this week. Alone.

He'd been hopeful, but he hadn't let himself ask until now. The two weeks they'd spent together after Adrienne and Will's wedding had been incredible. She was the smartest, funniest, sexiest woman he'd ever been with. It had been quite the pleasant surprise to find such an intriguing woman in such a small package. But to underestimate the spark inside that petite frame was a serious mistake. She was a firecracker in bed and out.

Their two weeks together had flown by, and before he knew it, he'd had to leave for New Orleans. Like all his relationships, it was short and without strings. Just a fun, sexy fling. But unlike most of the women he dated, Gwen hadn't wanted any more than that. She didn't eye his bank account or bare ring finger with burning ambition. She was just in it for a good time. He got the feeling she was busy, just as he was, and didn't want the complication of something serious. It was perfect.

So perfect he was hoping she'd be up for another round.

Apparently their short time together had not been enough for Alex to get his fill of Gwen. He typically grew bored with a woman after a few dates. If they pushed for more, he pushed the end button on his cell phone. He was always open about it, but most women seemed to think they might be the one to tame him. None had come close.

At best, Gwen had managed to stay on his mind amid the distractions. For the last seven months, Alex had been working on a new real estate development project in New Orleans that had sucked up a lot of his free time. Despite everything, thoughts of her would occasionally sneak into his brain while he was sitting in a boring meeting or lying in his bed at night. She'd even slipped into his thoughts as he'd trolled Bourbon Street. After their time together, it seemed that none of the women he met, especially in a setting like that, were up to par. Night after night he'd slink back to his hotel, alone.

Alex just couldn't shake the memory of Gwen. The soft caress of her hands across his stomach, the scent of her lavender shampoo, the sharp sass of her wit wrapped in the soft contrast of the Tennessee accent that came out when she was flustered...

Another week together ought to get her out of his system. Then he could get back on the prowl and reaffirm his reputation as a notorious bachelor.

Now that his project had gotten rolling, he could take a step back and let Tabitha and his management team run the show. When he and his friend Wade had started their first real estate development business, they'd been hands-on, start to finish. Now that he'd spun off and had the money to hire talented staff, he could do what he wanted and keep from getting bogged down in the details. He was looking forward to more time to play than he'd had in a long time. A few days in the Hamptons for the Fourth of July holiday was a great way to kick it off.

Alex turned onto the road that would lead to Will and Adrienne's waterfront vacation estate. Adrienne had concluded the family's ten-thousand-square-foot summerhouse was far too large for just the two of them and decided to make an event out of it. About eight other people would be joining them this week for some relaxation and fun.

At first, he hadn't planned to come, but when he realized Gwen would be there, too, he'd changed his mind. Although they'd agreed not to contact each other, there was a part of him that wished she had texted him every now and then. He missed the sound of her laughter and her bright smile. A few days with her could scratch that itch.

What he hadn't known until now was whether Gwen was bringing someone with her. He was hoping she would be up for Fling 2.0, but he couldn't be sure. If she'd shown up with another man, this would have been a long, boring week of clambakes, pool parties and cold beds.

A small, worn wooden sign marked the circular

driveway to the house. Alex slowed his Corvette and turned in, pulling behind a Range Rover and a silver Mercedes convertible.

He popped his fist against the horn to announce his arrival and climbed out of the car. His khakis and polo shirt had been a touch too warm in the city, but near the water there was a nice breeze making it cooler and much less humid. Perfect for being outside.

"Alex!" Adrienne called out from the front porch. "Will, Alex is here."

She started down the steps to greet him, and Alex noticed that his best friend's bride was looking as lovely as ever. She wore a pair of denim shorts with a light green sleeveless blouse tucked in, and her dark hair was pulled into a ponytail, her complexion a bit pink from the sun. To see her now, you'd never know she'd once survived a plane crash and undergone multiple reconstructive surgeries.

As Adrienne held out her arms to hug him, only the thin, white line of a scar up her left forearm remained. Alex pulled her into his embrace and gave her a tight squeeze. He'd been so busy lately he really hadn't seen much of them, either. In his business, it was feast or famine. Either he was working almost nonstop for months at a time, or he was home, freewheeling while his manager, Tabitha, handled the rest. The project in New Orleans was a big one and sucked up more of his time than he had expected.

"Do you need help with your bags?" she asked. "Will is out back fighting with the new grill."

The thought of Will grilling brought a smile to Alex's face. They'd likely starve or call in a caterer before the trip was over. "Nope," he said, pulling a duffel bag from the passenger's seat. "This is all I have."

"I'll show you to your room, then."

Alex followed Adrienne and her flip-flops into the house and up the grand, circular staircase that wrapped around the living room. They traveled down a long, white hallway with alternating doorways and artwork on each side.

"Here it is," she said, opening the door and waving him inside.

Alex went in and tossed his bag down on the queen-size sleigh bed that dominated the room. The bed was covered in an intricately designed quilt and large, fluffy pillows. The light oak wood of the bed matched the tall dresser and bedside stand. There was a flat-screen television, an overstuffed chair and ottoman, and a ceiling fan turning gently to keep air circulating. Honestly, it was far nicer than the hotel room he'd been living in the last few months in New Orleans, and he'd paid quite a bit for the privilege.

"You have your own bathroom," Adrienne said, gesturing toward a door on the far wall.

"Great. Where is everyone else staying?" Alex wanted to know exactly how far he might have to go in his underwear to get back from Gwen's room before everyone woke up. If he was lucky, it was her door he could see across the way.

"Emma, Peter and Helena are staying down the hall. Sabine, Jack and Wade are in those rooms across from you. Will and I have the suite downstairs, and Gwen's room is just off the kitchen."

Damn. She was about as far from his room as logistically possible. Just great. That would make sneaking around quite a bit more difficult. Alex tried not to frown. He didn't need Adrienne asking questions.

"Looks like I have everything I need, then."

"Great. I'll let you get settled, and we'll see you downstairs."

Adrienne slipped out of the room, leaving him alone. He heard the dull slap of her footsteps down the wooden staircase, then pulled back the curtains and watched for her to step out onto the patio. He could see Will out there, hovering over the stainless steel grill that was built into the L-shaped outdoor kitchen they'd added since his last visit. Adrienne kissed him on the cheek and assisted him in investigating the mysteries of the new cooktop.

With the coast clear, he unzipped his bag and pulled out a bottle of wine and a bundle of crimson roses he'd picked up for Gwen on his way out of town. His father had always taught him that a gift was never a bad way to start off on the right foot, especially with women. Alex would've gotten her some jewelry, but the last time he'd tried, she'd pretty much laughed in his face. To avoid a repeat, he'd opted for something a little more low-key. With Gwen, he'd learned he had to strike a balance between thoughtful, nice and too expensive.

Hiding them behind his back, he headed downstairs in search of Gwen's room. He'd stayed in that bedroom a few years back at another summertime Taylor gathering, so now he easily found it near the laundry room and kitchen, tucked away in a remote corner. At one time, it had been the maid's quarters.

The door was halfway open. From his vantage point, he could see an open suitcase lying on the bed. Alex approached the entry and poked his head around the corner. Gwen was putting clothes away in her dresser.

Her back was to him, so he took a moment to admire her. A strapless cotton sundress flowed in bright colors to her ankles and bare feet. Her curly, ash-blond hair was pulled up in a clip that left soft tendrils at her bare neck. He was suddenly filled with the undeniable urge to kiss her there.

Alex slipped silently into the room, creeping across the plush rug to come up behind her.

"Hello again, gorgeous," he said, wrapping his arms around her to display the wine and roses and planting a warm kiss at the apex of her neck and shoulder. "These are for you." He felt her tremble slightly at his touch, then stiffen beneath his hands.

She didn't turn to him or take the gifts. Instead, a soft, hesitant voice politely replied, "Hello, Alex."

A feeling of unease nagged at Alex's brain and threatened to override the longing building in his gut. This wasn't the welcome he'd expected from her at all. He'd anticipated a smile, a hug, maybe an enthusiastic "Hello, sugar"…or at the very least, a thank-you for the flowers. Perhaps he had miscalculated. Her less than enthusiastic greeting made him wonder if she was upset with him. Had she expected him to call even though they'd agreed not to? At the time, she'd seemed to understand what they had together, but she wouldn't be the first woman to be disappointed or upset when the relationship ended as planned.

She finally took the roses and the wine, setting them on top of the dresser without really looking at them, her back still facing him. Note to self—Gwen wasn't a fan of expensive jewelry, roses or red wine. What *did* she like?

"How have you been?" she asked. Her voice sounded more normal now, less timid. Perhaps he'd just startled her.

"Busy," he said, his free hands now planting at her waist. She didn't pull away, but she didn't lean back against him, either. The flowers hadn't done their magic, but he knew just how to thaw out a woman's cold reception. The feel of his arousal pressed against her back would certainly soothe her pride and let her know how badly she'd been missed. "You?" he asked, letting his palms glide around to her stomach to pull her reluctant body into him.

At least, that was the idea. As his hands ran over a soft, rounded belly instead of the flat, firm one he remembered, Alex paused.

The realization washed over him like a tidal wave. The breath was knocked from his lungs and his muscles seized, allowing him to neither pull away nor spin her around to see the truth with his own two eyes.

"Busy," she whispered, repeating his words. "And as you may have noticed, pregnant."

The hands on Gwen's rounded stomach had turned from a gentle caress to a grip of immovable stone in an instant. The pressing of his fingertips into her belly were almost painful in their intensity. She put her hands over his and pried them away so she could turn around and finally face him.

Gwen hadn't been sure how she would feel seeing Alex again. The boyishly handsome face was just as she remembered it, sending her heart racing unexpectedly in her chest. Her fingers itched to run through his messy, blond hair. Her lips ached to leave a trail of kisses along the faint stubble of his jaw. In an instant, it was as if the last few months apart had never happened.

But at the same time, Gwen wondered if coming here had been a mistake.

The golden-hazel eyes that had once sparkled with mischievous passion were now wide with unexpressed emotions and burrowing into her stomach. Granted, it was hard to ignore. To say she'd blossomed in the last month was an understatement. She'd gone from a small pooch of a belly to full-blown second trimester almost overnight.

But it wasn't the surprise on Alex's face that concerned her. She expected that. It was the red blotches spreading across his skin and the hard, angry line of his jaw. He was always so laid-back and carefree. She'd never seen him upset, but she supposed when you had enough money, you could fix any problem. Now his personality had taken a one-eighty swing, and Gwen wasn't even certain he'd taken a breath for the last two minutes.

"Breathe, honey, before you pass right out."

His gaze darted to meet hers, the intensity of it making her chest tight. She wanted to squirm and move away from him, but she stood her ground. She hadn't done anything wrong. Why should she run?

"Breathe?" he said at last. "You show up here pregnant without saying a word to me about it and tell me to breathe? Were you saving the news for my birthday or something?"

"It's none of your business what I do. We aren't an item. Why would I…?" Gwen started to argue, then stopped, realizing her mistake. She'd never thought for a minute that Alex would think this child was his. She was only five months along, but the furious set of his jaw indicated he wasn't familiar enough with a female gestational cycle to make that distinction.

They'd slept together and now she was pregnant. He'd obviously jumped to the wrong conclusion.

"This isn't your baby," Gwen quickly clarified.

Alex opened his mouth to start arguing with her, but her sudden and unexpected response stopped him short.

"Are you certain?" he asked, his face almost pained by the words.

"One hundred percent. I haven't seen you since November, and I'm only at twenty-two weeks. Unless some of your li'l swimmers decided to camp out in my apartment for the holidays and attack when I was least expecting it, you're in the clear."

His brow furrowed, and she could see the anger slowly fade away as the muscles in his neck relaxed. His whole body started to uncoil and he took a deep breath, the casual, easygoing posture she remembered finally gaining hold.

Alex ran a hand through the shaggy strands of his golden hair and shook his head. "You really scared the hell out of me, Gwen."

She was certain of that. Blended in with the anger glittering in his amber eyes had been a healthy dose of fear. When they were together, they'd been quite meticulous when it came to taking all the proper precautions. They both had their reasons. Alex said he didn't want the entanglement of a child, although she expected there was more to it than just that. And as for Gwen, well, she was sure he couldn't guess why it had been so important for her at the time, but an unexpected pregnancy would've derailed everything.

"I'm sorry," Gwen said, the words coming easier with the tension in the room fading. "If you were the father, I would've told you. I couldn't keep a secret like that for long, and Adrienne would've had my hide for even trying."

For her own self-preservation, Gwen had kept her fling with Alex a secret. Adrienne would make a bigger deal out of it than it was intended to be. And by the time her friend had returned from her honeymoon in

Bali, Alex was gone and there wasn't much point in mentioning it. It was just one fantastic last hoorah before her man-break. Nothing more.

Instead, she'd tried to pretend it never happened. The holidays and her pregnancy had done well to distract her. To a point. She blamed the hormones for her more emotional moments when thoughts of Alex slipped through her defenses.

Now Alex looked a touch uncomfortable, shifting his weight and burying his hands in the pockets of his khakis. It was about as close to repentant as she'd ever seen him. "I wish I'd known about all this," he said. "I mean, Will had no reason to think I would care, but I never would've touched you like that. Or brought you wine, obviously."

Gwen smiled. After eight months without a man, his brief touch had been the highlight of her week. Month, maybe. It was right up there with feeling the baby flutter inside her for the first time. "That's okay. Pregnancy isn't contagious."

Alex laughed, breaking the last of the nervous tension in her bedroom and reminding her of the lover she knew. During those two weeks, they'd spent as much time laughing and talking as they had making love. They'd walked around the city, dined in new restaurants and just enjoyed being in one another's company. It was easy to be with Alex.

Looking at him now with his bright, charming smile made her long to touch him again. For Alex to hold her and whisper into her ear the way he had before. But that was a pointless fantasy. Alex was just the latest in a long line of men destined not to stick around. As relationships went, Gwen had a miserable track record. She was always drawn to the men that would leave. A guy that was steady, loyal and committed to a woman didn't even show up on her radar. Probably because she didn't want one hanging around that long.

"That's not what I meant," he said. "I meant I shouldn't have presumed you were free for us to, uh... I mean, I hope if the father finds out about this that you let him know I didn't realize you were taken. Will said you came up alone."

Gwen frowned. "'Taken'?" Truth be told, she was anything but. Occupied, perhaps, but not taken.

Alex's glance darted to her left hand as it rested on the swell of her stomach. "I guess I assumed since you were having some guy's baby that he might mind me groping you. I know I'd probably be crazy with jealousy if someone put the moves on the mother of my child."

That was one thing Gwen certainly didn't have to worry about. "I assure you that Robert isn't really concerned with what I do or with whom."

In an instant, a touch of Alex's previous anger returned, and a dark pink colored the outer shell of his ears. His hazel gaze pinned her on the spot. "Robert who? Tell me the bastard's name."

Gwen's eyes widened in shock. She wasn't quite sure if it was because Alex looked as though he was ready to punch the baby's father in the face, or because he cared enough to go to the trouble. She thought she was just another notch in the proverbial bedpost. Certainly it wouldn't warrant such a protective response from him. "What does it matter? What are you going to do about it?"

"I'm going to sit him down and make sure he does right by you and his child."

"Good lord." Gwen laughed. "You sound like my Paw-Paw. Are you going to take your shotgun, too?"

"If I had one. I might go buy a gun just for the occasion."

Gwen's lower back was beginning to throb from standing in one place for too long. It was just one of the joys the second trimester had brought, along with insatiable hunger and an aching, expanding belly. A fair trade for the end of morning sickness, she supposed. She moved over to the bed to sit at the edge. "I appreciate the offer, but that won't be necessary. The situation is complicated and will take more than a few minutes to explain. But trust me when I tell you Robert is a perfectly wonderful husband and will be just as good a father."

"He's married? Jesus, Gwen. Maybe you need a talking-to as well."

Gwen sighed and patted the mattress beside her. "Sit down, Alex."

He hesitated for a moment, then settled down beside her. He maintained what he probably thought was the proper distance from a mother-to-be, but she could still feel the warmth of him, and the scent of his cologne hovered in the air she breathed. It took everything she had not to close her eyes and imagine being in his arms again. Not that she ever would be. Even if he had been interested initially, there was nothing quite like a surprise pregnancy to kill the mood.

"Listen, you've got the wrong idea about all of this. The father hasn't done anything wrong. In fact, his wife knows about everything and approves. Robert and Susan are good people who suffered a horrible tragedy that no one should ever have to face. I had the power to help them, so I did."

Alex watched her speak, visibly struggling to see where she was going with this. She understood the confusion. Her own mother hadn't approved, even when she had all the details. *Especially* when she had all the details. Only Adrienne, who knew Gwen was a marshmallow underneath her hard candy shell, could see why she had to do this for people who were practically strangers.

She took a deep breath. "I told you this wasn't your baby, but I didn't tell you the whole story. The truth is this isn't my baby, either."

Two

"I'm a surrogate."

Alex fully understood the meaning of the term, but somehow he couldn't connect it in his brain where Gwen was concerned. "This isn't your baby?"

"No. Someone else's bun is baking in my oven. I'm just a rental. This is Robert and Susan's baby biologically, and as soon as the adoption paperwork is filed, it will be theirs legally as well."

This was certainly unexpected. The pendulum of his emotions had swung wildly from one side to the other and back over the last few minutes. First, he was a father. Then he wasn't. Now she wasn't even a mother. He'd never anticipated that procreation could be this complicated. "Why would you agree to do something like that?"

Gwen shrugged. "Why wouldn't I? It wasn't like I was in a serious relationship or had other plans that would interfere. I spend a lot of my time at the hospital, and that's where I met them. Susan was a patient on my floor for several weeks after being in a severe car wreck in the Lincoln Tunnel. She was seven months pregnant at the time. Not only did she lose the baby, but she isn't able to carry another child. They were such a sweet couple, going through so much pain. How could I turn down the opportunity to help them?"

"You're being compensated, right?"

Gwen frowned, her nose wrinkling delicately. "Of course not. You sound like my mother. They're paying my medical expenses, but that's it. I didn't do this for the money, and frankly, they aren't in a position to pay even if it wasn't illegal. This isn't some fancy work-around for a rich, thin society woman who doesn't want to ruin her figure with pregnancy."

Alex wasn't quite sure what to say. She was a damn saint and probably the only woman on his roster who could come close to qualifying. He wasn't used to being around women like that. "Are you getting anything out of this other than a warm, fuzzy feeling?"

"Some distance," she said. "When I volunteered to do this, I decided I would use the time to take a break from relationships."

"So, what, you've sworn off men?"

Gwen smiled. "Yes, for now."

He wasn't quite sure what to say to that. He lived in a world where people of means indulged in whatever, whenever they wanted. Alex let his gaze drop to Gwen's hand as it rested on the soft swell of her stomach. Around her wrist was a silver charm bracelet with a heart-shaped lock charm. The one he'd bought her at Tiffany during their previous time together. "You're wearing your bracelet," he said.

Gwen smiled and held out her wrist to look at it. "I've worn it every day since you bought it for me."

Alex shook his head. He'd practically had to force the gift on Gwen. She'd finally chosen the bracelet under the threat of not leaving the store until she picked something. She'd refused diamond earrings. The roses and wine had been a complete failure. But at least she liked the bracelet.

"It's my chastity bracelet."

"What?" Alex nearly choked. "Like a chastity belt?"

"Slightly less medieval, but the same basic idea. I wear it as a reminder."

"You're using my gift as a reminder to avoid men? The irony is rich."

Gwen shrugged. "It was perfect timing. You insisted I buy something. I saw the lock charm in the case, and I knew it was the perfect symbol of the new journey I was starting on. A subtle reminder to stay on track, as if being pregnant wouldn't do that for me already. I mean, who'd want me like this? It was the perfect time to quit dating."

Alex was about to tell her that he, for one, would still want her, when Adrienne's voice in the kitchen caught their attention. "Gwen?" she called.

"You'd better go," Gwen said, standing quickly. She picked up the roses and wine from the dresser and thrust them back at him. "Take these with you. I don't want to explain where they came from."

Alex wasn't quite ready to leave, but he wasn't ready to explain to Adrienne why he was alone with Gwen, either. Jumping up, he stuck his head out the doorway toward the kitchen, then dashed off in the other direction. He rounded the corner into the living room unseen and opted to head back to his room to finish unpacking.

Or at least, to decompress. He'd had too big a shock in the last few minutes to go out onto the patio and be the life of the party just yet.

Talk about a game changer! For the most part, Alex thought he had women figured out. Between his mother and the list of ladies who had drifted in and out over his lifetime, he had a pretty solid understanding of the female of the species.

The exception was Gwen.

Somehow she took all his expectations and tossed them out the window. She was a genuinely good person. The first moment he'd laid eyes on her, she had been running herself ragged to make Will and Adrienne's wedding special. Later, he'd discovered she spent her working hours taking care of the sick, and from the looks of things now, she sacrificed her precious personal time for others, too. He couldn't imagine even one of the women he'd dated over the last ten years agreeing to anything like that. The majority of them were looking for some hedonistic pleasure or a sugar daddy. Either way, it was all about them. Selfish and spoiled, every last one of them. It was no wonder he never wanted to keep them around for long.

But Gwen...having a stranger's baby and asking for nothing in return? To subject her body to the ravages of childbearing without the benefit of having her own child when she was done? That wasn't exactly like loaning your neighbor a cup of sugar or donating an old coat to the homeless shelter. She was taking charity to a whole new level.

Alex slipped into his bedroom and shut the door behind him to block out the rest of the world. It wasn't until his weight sank down into the soft mattress that the rush of adrenaline coursing through his veins finally seemed to subside.

Gwen was a remarkable woman. Smart, funny, caring, but saint or no, Alex had to admit he was still relieved to find that wasn't his child. There were worse women in Manhattan to be bound to through the bonds of shared custody, but that had been close. Too close.

Since he'd started his heated pursuit of women, Alex had been nearly religious about using protection. It was the only way to shield himself. Not only from disease but from the women out there who would like nothing better than to have his child and a permanent connection to his bank accounts. The Stanton Steel company had made a fortune during the race to build railroads across the United States. The generations since then had done well investing it. And Alex was the sole heir to it all.

By necessity, his record with women was flawless. To the dismay of women everywhere, no one had conceived Alex Stanton's child. And for that, he was eternally grateful. He wasn't interested in the emotional, physical and financial entanglements. If his parents had taught him nothing else, they had shown him that marriage for the sake of a child made everyone miserable in the end. He had no intention of becoming a workaholic who bought his son's affections, like his father, or an emotionally abusive recluse like his mother, who blamed her son for her own wretched existence.

If he died single and childless, Alex would consider that a victory. He'd rather donate his fortune to charity just to hear the collective sound of the hearts of every ambitious socialite in Manhattan breaking.

And yet…for half a heartbeat when he'd thought Gwen was having his baby…there'd been this feeling he hadn't anticipated. Sure, he was angry with her for keeping it from him and sort of freaked out in general, but he'd also had a touch of excitement. He'd told himself after their weeks together that his thoughts of Gwen would fade. Continuing in any kind of real relationship with her would just lead to expectations he couldn't fulfill.

But in that moment, fate had very nearly made the decision for him. If that child was his, then perhaps Gwen could be, too. Not just a holiday fling, but something beyond that. Maybe they wouldn't have the kind of family pictured on Christmas cards, but there could be more than what they'd had. And he'd wanted it. The thought had flashed through his mind almost as quickly as his heart had raced in his chest.

And then it was gone.

Alex would never tell another living soul about his moment of weakness. Nor would he admit that, when she'd said the baby wasn't his, he'd felt a pang of regret and jealousy mingled in with the rush of relief.

What the hell was wrong with him?

Certainly he didn't require a baby as an excuse to have Gwen in his arms again. That was a life-changing complication he simply didn't need. But knowing that she was still single, albeit a bit preoccupied, meant his plans for this week hadn't completely fallen apart yet. If she was interested, they could still have a little fun and, hopefully, this time he'd be able to move on when it was over.

Alex heard a familiar melody of a woman's laughter from the patio. He strode to the window and pulled aside the curtain. Gwen had joined the others outside. She was standing near the sparkling turquoise pool, talking to Adrienne and another woman he didn't know.

He couldn't hear their conversation, but Adrienne spoke and Gwen laughed again.

He had missed that sound. When Gwen was really tickled, she laughed wholeheartedly. No polite, uptight chuckles from her. He loved how she could let herself go. Whether it was laughter or pleasure, she allowed herself to just feel it and react without worrying what other people thought. As he watched, her head tipped back and she giggled in unrestrained amusement. Her eyes closed, her white smile flashing up at him. Her movement allowed the golden sunlight to highlight the creamy expanse of her chest and shoulders exposed by her dress.

Alex had been too preoccupied earlier to notice how Gwen had changed since he had seen her in November. Last year, long hours at the hospital and attempts to diet before the wedding had trimmed her petite frame to the point of being almost too thin, in his opinion. Women always worried too much about those last few vanity pounds. In his experience, a woman with curves and a healthy appetite was more fun both in bed and out.

Now, as he watched her from the window, he could see Gwen was obviously pregnant, but everything about her seemed to be softer and more welcoming. Her skin radiated a rosy, maternal glow. Her breasts were fuller and her hips a touch rounder. Pregnancy really suited her.

And him.

The fire in his gut that had been building since he had gotten into the car this morning returned. The shock of their previous discussion had dulled it, but now it was back with renewed fervor. The woman he'd fantasized about for months was here, looking more beautiful than he remembered. Standing in the sunlight with her long, flowing dress, she looked more like some ancient Greek fertility goddess than a nurse.

The tightness in his groin forced him to shift his stance uncomfortably. Alex was surprised by his visceral reaction to her. There was something primal piqued by her new, soft curves. Typically the sight of a pregnant woman threw up red flags declaring her off-limits. It was something he'd never considered, given he never planned to settle down and start a family.

But Gwen wasn't off-limits. Her situation was unique and certainly complicated, but he didn't see any barriers between them. If she could be coaxed into continuing their affair, they could spend another fantastic week in bed together. Alex wanted that week to start as soon as possible.

"Sworn off men, have you, Gwen? We'll just see about that."

Letting the curtain drop, he headed downstairs to join the party and begin his heated pursuit of Gwen Wright.

"About damn time!" Will shouted toward the house.

Gwen turned that direction in time to see Alex strut onto the blue flagstone patio that arched out from the house. The tall, white pergola that lined the back of the house was covered in clematis vines this time of year, and it shaded almost everything below. Patches of dark and light danced across his face as he approached the outdoor kitchen, where everyone had congregated.

"The party can officially start," he announced, giving Gwen a brilliant smile before he bent down to pull a cold bottle of locally microbrewed beer out of the small refrigerator inset to the right of the grill.

The small gesture brought a wave of warmth to her

cheeks that had nothing to do with the sun. Perhaps she'd worried for nothing. When Adrienne had first invited her up here for the Independence Day holiday, she'd had doubts. Her friend had promised her a relaxing vacation by the ocean with nothing but fun and friends. It sounded like a dream.

The time away from work would be a godsend, as would going a couple days without having to climb the four flights of stairs to her apartment. Her daily routine got rougher as each week ticked by. She couldn't imagine what it would be like in the last few months. She needed this break more than she'd realized.

But she'd known seeing Alex again would be awkward. Her being pregnant made it doubly so. It wasn't because they had parted on bad terms. They had both known it was nothing more than a little short-term fun. He'd had a business trip to go on, and it had seemed like the right time to end whatever they had going. But once he was gone, she'd been left with this restless, icky feeling she'd never felt before.

Eventually the complications of her life had put those concerns out of her head, but it had just confirmed some of the thoughts she'd been having about her choices in men. As in—she always made bad ones. Alex was no different. And it just wasn't working for her anymore. The decision to take the next year off from dating was obviously a wise choice.

But Alex didn't know how she felt about things. Their relationship had ended on a positive note as far as he was concerned. And given the firm arousal that had pressed into her back less than an hour ago, he'd arrived alone and interested in having another go at it.

At least he *had*. Until twenty-two weeks of belly had come between them. Now he probably thought she was

as sexy as a beluga whale—or worse in Alex's mind—
a pregnant woman.

It was probably for the best. There was a reason
why she'd planned her man-break to coincide with the
pregnancy. It was built-in willpower. And lately, she'd
needed it. The months of celibacy and the second-tri-
mester hormones had done a number on her libido. If
Alex was still interested, she'd be tempted to use him
for a couple nights of hot sex, the way he used every
other woman in his life. Turnabout was fair play, right?

But, fortunately, she didn't have to worry. Alex would
stay at arm's length from her all week, and she wouldn't
need the strength necessary to turn him down. And
she *would* have to turn him down. She'd done so well.
She didn't want to fall off the wagon, even for a guy
like Alex.

"Alex, have you met everybody?" Adrienne set down
her glass of tea on the table and began fulfilling her role
as hostess by introducing her guests.

Gwen had heard it all before, but she listened a second time in the hope she would actually retain the in-
formation. First was Emma, Adrienne's half sister of
sorts. She was actually the child of George and Pauline Dempsey, who had lost their older daughter in the
same wreck that had nearly killed Adrienne. They'd
unofficially adopted Adrienne and let her take Emma
shopping or on trips from time to time. Emma had just
graduated from high school, and when she got home,
she had to pack up and get ready for her freshman year
at Yale.

Next was Sabine, a somewhat funky twentysome-
thing who managed Adrienne's boutique. She had a nose
piercing and a bright purple stripe in her black hair, so

Gwen wasn't quite sure what to make of her. Adrienne ran in diverse circles.

Peter and Helena were a middle-aged couple who lived in the brownstone next to Will and Adrienne's new place on the Upper West Side. Rounding off the crowd was Wade, one of Will and Alex's friends from Yale and Alex's former business partner, and Jack, an editor for one of the big New York publishing houses. Apparently he had worked with Will at the paper a few years back.

It was a blur of names and faces that Gwen would forget the minute the next name was called. She'd blame her short-term memory loss on the pregnancy—it was easy to label almost anything as a symptom of her condition—but the truth of the matter was that she was simply bad with names. At work, it was easy. All the staff had name tags, and all the patients had their names on a plaque outside their door or a clipboard hanging at the foot of their bed.

When the introductions were finished, she decided her time standing in the sun was over. It had felt good at first, but now she was a minute or two from starting to burn. Taking her glass of iced tea, Gwen returned to the shade of the pergola and sat down on one of the cushioned Adirondack chairs.

Leaning back into the cool comfort of her chair, she instantly felt better. Thank goodness she wasn't full-term in the heat of the summer. Gwen wasn't sure she could bear that. Her apartment didn't have central air, just a small unit in the bedroom window. Most of the time she was cold natured and it suited her fine, but she'd had fire running through her veins the last few months.

Taking a refreshing sip of the sweet tea she'd brewed earlier, she watched the men gather around the grill.

Apparently millionaires could run companies and build empires, but outdoor cooking was a challenge. She watched Alex open the cabinet beneath it and make some adjustments to the propane line. A few minutes later, a roar of success sounded from the group.

"We have fire!" the editor guy—Jack?—shouted triumphantly.

Adrienne patted them all on the back and headed toward the house. "I'm off to prepare the meat," she said with a smile as she slipped inside.

Sabine with the purple hair quickly grew bored with the sight of an operating gas grill and came to sit in the shade with Gwen. They hadn't spoken much since she'd arrived. She was sure the woman was perfectly nice— Adrienne was a good judge of people—but Gwen just didn't know what they had in common to discuss.

"When are you due?" Sabine asked before taking a sip from her beer.

"Mid-October," Gwen said, although watching the other woman made her think the day couldn't come soon enough. Of all the lifestyle changes she'd had to make, the hardest had been giving up her favorite beer. She didn't drink much, but there was just something soothing about popping the top on a cold one after a long shift, plopping onto the couch and watching a few hours of reality television on her DVR.

"My son will be two in October, so I understand where you're at. Do you know what you're having yet?"

Gwen tried not to look too surprised to learn Sabine was a mother. Imagining her own mother with purple hair was just impossible. "A little girl. I had the ultrasound last week."

Susan and Robert had been over the moon in the doctor's office. It was hard to see the fuzzy image on the screen from her vantage point, but she tried not to be too disappointed. This was their baby after all, not hers. They did give her a copy of the latest ultrasound picture to show off. Unfortunately, it was in her purse on her bed when she needed it.

"Do you have any names picked out yet?"

The more pregnant Gwen became, the more of these questions she had to field. It had been easy when no one could tell she was pregnant. Now, unless it was just a quick comment from a stranger on the subway, it was best to tell them about her situation before they pressed on.

"No, actually, I'm a surrogate, so the baby techni-cally isn't mine to name. I think her parents are con-sidering Caroline Joy and Abigail Rose. Every time I talk to them they've changed it again. For now I just call her Peanut, because that's what she looked like on the first sonogram."

Sabine's eyes had grown wider as Gwen talked. Ap-parently dropping a detail like that and carrying on without pause had thrown her off her guard. "A sur-rogate? Wow. I don't think I could ever do that," she finally said.

"Why is that?"

"Being pregnant is such a life-changing experience. Whether or not the child is yours, you're going to bond with it. To go through months with that baby inside you and then to give it away... I just couldn't do it."

Gwen tried not to frown at Sabine. She probably didn't realize how her words would affect her. But they struck a chord. Gwen had never been interested in hav-ing a family of her own. She'd spent too much of her childhood being pushed aside by her mother when a new man came into her life. She wasn't about to do that to a child of her own. Acting as a surrogate seemed like an intriguing opportunity. Since she'd never thought she'd have kids, she'd never thought she would experience pregnancy.

Never once did she consider that she'd form an emotional attachment to another person's child. But Sabine was right. She'd underestimated what it was like to have life growing inside her. The moment she'd felt the first flutter in her stomach, Peanut had become a real person to her. She'd gotten in the habit of talking to the baby when she was alone in her apartment. She was the one who helped Gwen pick out what she would have for lunch. The silent child had become her main companion when her crowd of bar-hopping friends didn't know how to act around her anymore.

Gwen hadn't really realized it until that moment, but she *had* bonded with the baby. With four more months to go, how much worse would it get? She didn't even want to think about it. She was too prone to getting emotional lately.

Confused, she turned away from Sabine and found Alex watching her from across the patio. He was leaning casually against one of the white wooden posts, while either Jack or Wade, she couldn't be sure, talked to him. But he wasn't looking at them or even pretending to. He was looking at her. There was an intensity in his hazel eyes, but there was something different there than the desire he'd directed at her in the past. It almost felt like admiration, although she had no idea why Alex would look at her that way. She was pregnant, broke and overworked. That was no condition to admire.

"He is one sexy piece of man," Sabine commented, still oblivious to the effect her words had on Gwen.

The comment startled Gwen into turning back to the

woman beside her. Sabine's gaze was focused exactly in Alex's direction. Gwen had no claim to him, but the thought of him and Sabine together brought on a surge of jealousy that chased away the last of her confusing emotions. She opted to play dumb. "Who? Wade?"

"No, the guy who came late. Alex."

"Ahh," Gwen said, not trusting herself to comment further without sounding either bitter or jealous to the other woman's ears.

"Pity for me, but I think he's into you."

That perked Gwen's attention. Her head snapped toward him, but he had returned to his conversation. "Why would you say that?"

"Because he keeps watching you."

"Maybe I'm just funny-looking." She sighed.

"Nope," Sabine said with certainty. "When you're not watching, he's looking at you like you're the sweetest strawberry tart in the bakery window. He definitely wants a taste."

Gwen subconsciously stroked her rounded stomach and shook her head. "I appreciate you thinking so, but somehow I doubt he wants to take a bite out of this."

At that, Sabine cracked a crooked, knowing grin. "Oh, he does," she assured.

"Well, even if that were true, my life is a little complicated right now. I'm not interested."

Sabine laughed and shook her head. "I hardly think that matters. I've had my share of experience with those rich, cocky types. They get what they want, and they don't care who they have to roll over in the process. If I were you, I'd let him have his way with you. And let me tell you something if you don't already know. Between all the hormones and the increased blood flow, sex in the second trimester can be absolutely mind-blowing.

I bet that in the experienced hands of a man like Alex, you can multiply that by ten at least."

Gwen's jaw dropped open, but she didn't have the words to respond. Instead, she shifted her gaze back to Alex. This time he was watching her, and his obvious, heated appraisal was enough to send a surprising surge of desire down her spine.

Well, hell. She hadn't counted on him still being attracted to her. That certainly complicated things.

Willpower, she reminded herself as she sucked in a deep breath and began fidgeting with her bracelet. She was on a man-break, and Alex was just the kind of man who had necessitated the break to begin with. Her attraction to him was nothing more than hormones and months of celibacy conspiring against her. But she could fight it. She had to. It didn't matter what Alex wanted. He couldn't just snap his fingers and get his way.

And yet, as she looked at him across the patio, Gwen was fairly certain her celibacy streak was on the verge of coming to a wild, passionate end.

Three

By the time Gwen had taken the last bite of her dinner, she thought she might literally burst. She'd recently regained her appetite, and everything tasted so good, she couldn't help herself. She'd had a grilled chicken breast and a cheeseburger in addition to the array of sides Adrienne had prepared. She was stuffed.

At least for an hour or so.

Given that Alex was watching her with his predatory gaze the whole time, she probably should've curbed her ravenous appetite and picked delicately at her food, but Peanut would have her way. After a rough first trimester living on saltines and lemon-lime soda, the hunger and the ability to keep it down were welcome. Even if the extra pounds were not. The doctor said she was right on track with her weight gain, but after a lifetime of trying to get smaller, not bigger, it was hard to change how she thought about things.

After they were done eating, several of the ladies started rounding up dishes, and the guys went inside for what promised to be a rowdy and high-stakes game of poker. Gwen scooped up her plate and a nearby bowl of potato salad and followed the other women into the kitchen.

"What are you doing?" Helena chided, snatching the items away from her the moment she crossed the threshold into the house. "You need to rest."

Gwen frowned. "I'm pregnant, not paralyzed. If washing dishes is hazardous to my condition, someone needs to tell me, because I've been doing it the whole time."

"Of course not. But take the opportunity to relax for once," Adrienne said, brushing past her with a platter and another bowl. "We can handle it."

The cherry-and-granite kitchen was quite large, but even Gwen realized that the four women already in there were bumping elbows and dancing around to clean up. A fifth one with a protruding belly probably wouldn't be much help.

With a sigh, she snatched one of her favorite peppermint candies from the bag she left on the counter, turned, and went back outside. The sun had set, but the sky was still bright with orange-and-red hues streaking across it. Beyond the pool and the expansive lawn that extended on both sides of the house, she spied the boathouse and pier that led out into the harbor.

A walk would probably help things settle, she decided. She slipped out of her sandals and kicked them to the side, then headed across the perfectly manicured lawn. The blades of grass were soft and cool, welcoming the bottoms of her feet to sink into them. It was a beautiful evening, one like she hadn't experienced in a long time. Along the tree line, she could see the blinking dance of fireflies as they appeared for the night. The breeze coming off the water was warm and salty, mingling with the scent of freshly mown grass.

It reminded her of her home in Tennessee. There, of course, the water was the creek that ran behind her grandparents' house, but the grass and the flashing lightning bugs were just the same. She had the urge to climb into the tire swing her Paw-Paw had hung for her and sway for hours, as she used to.

For a brief moment, Gwen was overcome with homesickness. She loved Manhattan—the energy, the excitement, the culture. But it had never felt like home to her. It made her wonder if she ever would've left Tennessee if it hadn't been the only way to get away from her mother. Following a guy she barely had lukewarm feelings for wasn't very smart, but it was a sure ticket out of her mother's clutches.

In the end, she and Ty went their separate ways, but she had gotten what she wanted from him—about six hundred miles of breathing room and her very own apartment, albeit tiny.

Gwen reached the pier and opted to walk out to the edge and watch the water. The occasional boat would sail by and send a ripple across the surface, but for the most part, the water was calm and still this time of day. At the end of the rough, wooden planks, she sucked in a lungful of ocean air and sighed.

She enjoyed getting away from the chaos more than she'd expected. There was a serenity out here that seemed to sink into her bones and force her muscles to unknot. Even Peanut had settled down and stopped squirming around. It was a shame she wasn't in the right tax bracket to live out here. She'd have to take a job as a live-in nurse for some old, rich Hamptons resident to do that. Unfortunately, caring for an entitled hypochondriac didn't really work for her.

Perhaps, after the baby was born, she should give some more thought about going back to Tennessee. That would probably make it easier on everyone with no awkward, obligatory visits. Robert and Susan could just take their baby and continue life as it was before their accident, and Gwen could return to the life she knew and start fresh.

The black, still waters around her beckoned. She couldn't remember the last time she'd been in a body of water that wasn't chlorinated, and she wanted to put her feet in it. Easing back, she sat on the boards and pulled her dress up to her knees. The water was cool and refreshing as she slipped her bare feet in to just above the ankles.

Looking out, she realized, as she had every time the idea of moving home hit, that going back to Tennessee really wasn't an option, as nice as all this seemed. For one thing, her romanticized memories of home would never hold up to reality. Paw-Paw and Gran were dead, and their old farmhouse and cornfields had been leveled to put up a housing subdivision. Returning would mean an apartment in Knoxville, which was a pretty sizable city, especially when the University of Tennessee, her alma mater, was in session.

And for another thing, she'd have to deal with her mother. She wasn't a powerless five-year-old girl anymore, but the less angst Gwen had to handle, the better.

Cheryl Wright was a desperate single mom on a never-ending quest for love.

When her relationships were going well, Gwen had been in the way and would get shipped off to her grandparents. When the relationship fell apart, Gwen would come home and take care of the house, as her mother was too distraught to get out of bed for days at a time. As Gwen got older, she was really more of a housekeeper than a daughter, although a housekeeper wouldn't have to hear about how she was the reason her mother couldn't keep a man.

Ever the expert, her mother had given Gwen an earful when she'd told her she was moving to New York City with Ty. He was a no-good loser just like her father, she'd warned. Of course, her mother was probably more concerned about who would make her dinner than Gwen's emotional health. Either way, it didn't matter. Gwen was gone and she couldn't go back.

With a sigh, she gazed across the harbor at a sailboat passing through. The mast was lined with white lights that twinkled across the surface as it moved. The boat called to her and made her want to swim out to it. Maybe she could convince the captain to take her on as first mate and she could just sail away from her problems. It seemed like a solid enough plan. That's what she'd done by coming to New York, minus the boat.

And that was why returning to Tennessee would feel like a defeat. Even though it would have nothing to do with Ty, her mother would get too much satisfaction from telling her she was right. Her life in Manhattan was hectic, but exciting. She worked at one of the top hospitals in the country and got to help so many people. She'd built a life for herself here over the past five years. She had friends. She was happy. At least until recently.

About a year ago, after another failed and mostly pointless relationship, she'd started having this nagging feeling that something was missing from her life. She didn't know what. Gwen had never wanted to chase the marriage and family that eluded her mother. But at the same time, whatever she was doing wasn't working, either. She was content, most days, but never really happy.

That's what her man-break was all about. A year off from the roller coaster of her dating life. Her hope was that, by the time it was over, she'd have a better idea of what she wanted. With four months left in her pregnancy, she was still pretty clueless on that front.

"You know, I hear sharks like to come up into these cooler waters and feed on the toes of pregnant women. It's a delicacy in their culture. Like sushi."

Gwen would've been startled, but she'd heard the faint tread of his footsteps on the planks of the pier. She didn't bother to turn around and look at him. "No. Everyone knows they all go to Florida for the holiday. It's like a buffet down there. Nothing hits the spot like a suntanned boogie boarder."

"Hmm. Quantity over quality, then." Alex sat down alongside her, crossing his legs to keep his khakis, loafers and argyle socks from getting wet. "What are you doing out here all by yourself?"

"I got banned from the kitchen by the other ladies, so I went for a walk and ended up out here. Why aren't you in there playing poker?"

Alex shrugged and looked across the harbor. "It's not really my game. I might as well just hand them each a couple thousand dollars and be done with it." With a smile he turned to her. "I'd kick their asses at racquetball, though."

Gwen smiled back. She'd always thought of Alex as more athletic and outgoing, so she wasn't surprised he could whip a bunch of corporate types at any kind of physical activity. His endurance was incredible. She blushed at the thought and hoped the rapidly darkening evening would disguise it. She didn't want to give him any more encouragement.

"So, how have you been lately? Aside from pregnant and all? We didn't really get to talk much earlier."

"I've been okay." She shrugged dismissively. "Work always takes up a lot of time. Preparing for the baby was a big deal, too. Lots of doctor visits and paperwork. It's a lot more complicated than just getting pregnant the old-fashioned way."

"And not nearly as fun, I'd wager," Alex said, leaning conspiratorially into her.

Gwen sighed. "No, not at all. Sadly, it's been so long, I can hardly draw much of a comparison."

Alex wrapped an arm around her shoulder and tugged her against his side. "Why has my lovely Gwen suffered such a long dry spell? I find it hard to believe."

"You flatter me," she said, shaking her head. "For one thing, they pumped me so full of hormones to get ready for the surrogacy that a man could've held a door for me and gotten me pregnant. Sex was out of the question. It was also the wrong time to start up anything serious. Do you wait until the third or fourth date to tell a man you can't go out next week because you'll be busy getting pregnant?"

"The fourth, definitely." Alex grinned. "But now that the deed is done, aren't you free to try dating again?"

Gwen couldn't suppress a chuckle. "In theory, but dating? Do you see this?" She looked down and pointed at her stomach. "This is man-repellant. And I'd be afraid of the men that *are* interested in me at this point. They might have some creepy pregnancy fetish, and that's the last thing I need."

Alex put a finger under her chin, tipped Gwen's face up to him and pinned her in place with his intense gaze.

"Let me assure you that nothing about you is repellant, and I'm most certainly a man."

The light mood instantly changed. A sizzle of electricity spanned the small gap between them, and Gwen could feel the beat of her heart thumping wildly in her chest.

Darkness had blanketed them, but she could still see the lights of the harbor reflecting in his eyes and the silver glow the moonlight cast across one side of his face. He was a beautiful man. Gwen would never say so—it wasn't the kind of thing he would want to hear—but it was true. Something about the lines and angles of his face drew her interest. His wide, disarming smile and mischievous eyes pulled her in. The shaggy, loose strands of his golden hair made her palms itch to run through them.

Alex was like some rogue angel in a painting that should be hanging in a museum somewhere. Perfect, alluring and untouchable.

He was so close. A part of Gwen wanted to lean in and kiss him. To take Sabine's advice and use Alex for all he was worth. The other part of her knew it would just mess with her mind.

Instead, Gwen rested her head on his shoulder, indulging in the comfortable cocoon of being in his arms again and making it impossible for her to kiss him. "And on top of everything," she said, pointedly ignoring his words, "I told you earlier I've sworn off men until after the baby is born. Being with you was my one last hoorah before all this," she said, rubbing her stomach. "I needed some time to myself."

Alex had watched the moonlight and shadows accentuate the battle going on inside Gwen's head until she finally hid from view. Unlike the Botoxed beauties he was usually bombarded with, she was the kind of woman whose every thought or feeling was plastered across her face. She didn't even try to disguise it, which made him wonder if she even knew. He wasn't going to let her hide from him. Not tonight.

"Stop," he whispered.

She sat up and frowned, a pout thrusting her full lower lip out to tease him. "What do you mean, 'stop'?"

"Stop using this pregnancy as an excuse to push people away. It won't work on me."

Gwen swallowed hard, her dark eyes widening slightly as she searched for meaning in his face. Apparently she was clueless about how transparent she was. Or how much attention he'd really paid to her when they were together before. "I don't know what you're—"

"You want me," he interrupted. "And I want you just as badly as I did all those months ago. There's nothing wrong with that. There's no reason to try to defuse the attraction between us just because of some artificial barrier you've put in place. If you want me, give in to your feelings."

She opened her mouth to argue, but his words seemed to have struck her temporarily mute. Alex thought this might be his opportunity to finally kiss her again the way he ached to, but she recovered more quickly than he'd hoped.

"What's your angle, Alex?"

He eased back a little, an eyebrow arching suspiciously at her. "Angle?"

"Yes. We both know I'm not the type of woman you usually go for. I'm not some tall, thin, surgically enhanced glamazon with aspirations of marrying well. Last time I was looking pretty good, but now I'm pregnant and celibate. Both are adjectives that fly in the face of everything you hold dear. I haven't been to a salon in months or splurged on a new outfit that wasn't from a maternity store. What are you getting out of this?"

Alex smiled his most mischievous grin and gazed into her eyes in the way that sent most women melting into his arms. "It hasn't been that long since we spent those fantastic few weeks together. Unless the hormones have scrambled your memory, I think we both know full well what benefit I'd be getting out of this."

Gwen's cheeks flushed red, her gaze breaking from his to look down at her hand as it rested on her stomach. "What we had last year was great, but I don't understand why you're putting the moves on me. Again. Especially considering everything else going on. Have you alienated every woman of consenting age in Manhattan? Are you that hard up?"

Alex snorted. "Hardly." There were plenty to choose from, in New York and New Orleans. He just hadn't found any that caught his attention as Gwen did.

"Then why me?" She looked up at him, a challenge in her dark brown eyes.

She honestly didn't think she was his type. Fortunately, Alex had a very broad and adventurous palate where women were concerned. But even then, Gwen was a beautiful, smart, funny, caring woman. What about that was unappealing to a secure and confident man? It sounded as though her experiences with less than worthy men had planted unwarranted doubts in her mind. She wouldn't need a break from men if she'd been involved with decent ones.

"Why not?" he retorted. "The two weeks we spent together were fun. Neither of us had any overly romantic ideas about what was going on. It was a perfect fling from start to finish. One of the many things I like about you, Gwen, is that you don't want more from me. So many women think they're going to change me, somehow. But I'm not about to tie myself down and be miserable for the rest of my life. With you, I feel like I can put my defensive walls down, relax and have a good time. To me, there's nothing sexier."

"Well, hell." Gwen looked as though she had a smart retort ready, but his explanation put all of it aside. "Alex, I—"

He charged in, capturing her mouth with his own and smothering any words. Gwen was stiff against him for just a moment of surprise, then her reservations were silenced and she gave in to the kiss. She softened, leaning forward to mold against him and bring her hand up to gently caress his face.

She tasted just like Christmas. She'd told him once that she kept handfuls of hard peppermint candies in the pockets of her scrubs at work. Gwen almost always had one in her mouth. He'd nearly forgotten until the spice assaulted his tongue and lured him to explore further.

Alex placed his hand on her hip and allowed it to slide up her side, pulling her as close to him as their position on the pier would allow. His fingertips stroked her heated skin through the thin, cotton fabric of her sundress. The touch coaxed a soft moan from her mouth.

Her encouragement made him bolder. His right hand glided up higher to cup the full swell of her breast. This time, his own groan of pleasure muffled hers. She was so much fuller and rounder than the last time he'd touched her. She was like a juicy, ripe peach in his hands, ready to be devoured. He couldn't wait to taste every inch of her and remind himself of anything he may have forgotten about Gwen in the last few months.

"Stop."

It was the word no man wanted to hear when he was caressing a woman's breast, but the soft whisper couldn't be ignored. Alex reluctantly pulled away, their warm breath still lingering in the space between them. He expected Gwen to distance herself, since she had called the cease-fire, but even she seemed hesitant to let the moment between them pass just yet.

"Why?" he asked, leaning his forehead against hers and closing his eyes.

"I just… I can't do this, Alex."

With a sigh, Alex moved away and unfolded his legs to stand on the pier. He reached down and took Gwen's hands in his own. The touch of her skin sent a tingle across his palms and up his arms, tightening every muscle in his body with anticipation. Gwen eased her feet out of the water and planted them firmly on the wooden planks as he pulled her up.

Instead of letting go, he tugged the full length of her body against him for one last touch, one last kiss, in the hope she might change her mind.

He'd forgotten she was pregnant until the only part of her body to make contact was the press of her breasts and the round curve of her belly. Their positioning was suddenly awkward, both of them pausing to see what had halted the progress of their physical connection.

The heated moment between them suddenly disintegrated as Gwen looked down and started giggling. "See, I told you. It is quite literally man-repellent." She brought a hand up to cover her mouth, but there was no stopping her contagious laughter once she got started.

What she didn't know was that her laughter was as

big a turn-on as anything else about her. Gripping her face with both hands, he leaned down and kissed her again.

The laughter silenced immediately as she stiffened in his arms. She didn't pull away, but she didn't give in to the kiss the way she had the first time, either. There was a hesitation in her touch, even as the smashed orbs of her breasts against the hard wall of his chest made him wild with arousal.

When she refused to give in, Alex pulled away and shook his head. He didn't understand how she could deny herself something they both wanted. This situation didn't need to be as complicated as she was making it. But he wasn't giving up on this seduction. Eventually he would convince her that he was right. This time Gwen took her own step back, looking up at him with confused black eyes that twinkled with the lights of the house. Her breath was ragged, every rise and fall of her chest tempting him with her out of his reach.

"I'm sorry. I just can't. Good night, Alex," she said. At that, she turned and walked back down the pier alone, disappearing into the night.

Four

Gwen awoke the next morning to the sounds of voices in the kitchen. Rolling onto her side, she picked up her watch from the nightstand and groaned. It was after nine. How had she slept so late?

She knew. Tossing and turning until well past three in the morning probably had something to do with it. But she just couldn't sleep. Her mind was still racing from her kiss with Alex. Every time she closed her eyes, she could see his smile. Every breath she sucked into her lungs was laced with his scent.

There was no getting away from Alex and how badly she wanted him. Break or no break, she couldn't help her reaction to him. Her body remembered his touch, and the taste she got last night wasn't nearly enough to soothe the need he easily built inside her.

But last night also brought the memories of their time together back in full Technicolor. As much fun as their fling had been, it had worked then because she was in a different place. An uncomplicated place.

Wanting Alex didn't change the fact that the kiss on the pier was a mistake. A fantastic, soul-stirring, spine-tingling mistake. She couldn't take it back, but she could keep things from going any further.

If she was that desperate for sex, she should try throwing herself at Wade or Jack. Or the first guy she could find once she returned to the city. Just not Alex. Giving in to him would be a bad idea. It might not seem like it at first, especially when the rush of his touch surged through her veins, but before the last of the holiday fireworks exploded, so would what they had together.

This time, she just knew it would end badly. The pregnancy had made her more emotional than normal. She didn't want to make the mistake of letting herself get too attached. Gwen could easily let herself get swept into some kind of fantasy. Out of all her past lovers, Alex was the least likely to stick around. Normally, that would be okay, but at this time in her life, there was no point in even starting something when finishing it would be so difficult.

Gwen ran her hand over her belly, pressing her palm in on one side to feel the baby stirring. "When you grow up, you be sure not to fall for a man like Alex, Peanut. You deserve the kind of man that will stick around and offer more than just sex and some flashy gifts. That's not enough."

She felt Peanut roll in response, then drive an elbow or a foot or something squarely into her bladder. Apparently she disagreed. The move sent Gwen leaping out of bed and scurrying into the bathroom. It was just as well. The day needed to begin, and Peanut was ready to go even if she wasn't.

Last night Will had mentioned something about VIP tickets they'd gotten everyone for a charity polo tournament today. It was supposedly one of the highlights of the trip, and she had no doubt they'd paid a small fortune for it. Both he and Alex had played on the Yale team in college, and everyone was gushing about how great it would be. Adrienne and Helena were putting together a gourmet picnic for dinner at the field. Emma had paraded around in a variety of hats, getting everyone's opinion on which one she should wear. It seemed like a big deal to the others.

Gwen knew very little about sports outside of college football. She was Southern, after all, so a basic knowledge of college football was provided by her father in her DNA. She occasionally followed the basketball team and even spent a semester as a little sister to the swim team, but that was about it where athletics were concerned.

Polo was up there with croquet and badminton in the "obscure sports for rich people" category. In the last two years of her friendship with Adrienne, they'd both undergone a sort of baptism by fire into Manhattan society. Neither was used to being around these kinds of social situations. Adrienne had adapted fairly well. Gwen still struggled, but she quickly learned there were few things rich people liked more than horses and wine. This polo tournament was sponsored by a large, prestigious winery, so it was the best of both for those who cared. No matter what situation Adrienne dragged her into, a basic knowledge of equestrian activities and how the rainfall was in Napa this year could save her from an awkward night out.

But the polo match should be fun anyway. She missed the energy and roar of excitement of UT football games, although she knew this would hardly come close.

By the time she emerged from her room, showered and dressed, the rest of the house was up and about as well. Several of the ladies were outside on the patio, but Gwen opted to crawl up onto one of the barstools in the kitchen and keep Adrienne company while she straightened up.

"Good morning, mama," Adrienne said with a smile. "Did you sleep well?"

"Yes," she lied. "Did I miss breakfast?"

"Not at all. The guys got up early to play a couple holes of golf, so they ate a long time ago. The rest of us just finished." Adrienne pulled out a plate and scooped some scrambled eggs, bacon, fruit salad and a biscuit onto it. "Here you go. I used your grandmother's biscuit recipe, and everyone was raving about them."

The scent was heavenly. Gwen started eating, washing the tasty bites down with the glass of milk Adrienne poured. Normally she hated milk, but it was just one more sacrifice she was making for Peanut's welfare.

"When do we leave for the polo match?" she asked.

"It doesn't start until four, but we have to drive to Bridgehampton for it, and I'm sure the men will want to arrive early. We've got plenty of time if there's something you wanted to do today."

Gwen shrugged. "Actually, I'm happy to do nothing. I just wasn't sure when I needed to be ready."

Adrienne smiled and leaned onto the counter. "I think you should make the most of doing nothing while you can. That's what this whole week is about. I know polo isn't your thing. You don't have to go to the match if you don't want to."

"Don't be silly," Gwen chided. "Of course I'll go. I don't even want to know how much those tickets cost you, so I'm not about to waste one. Anyway, anything we do here is better than working a twelve-hour shift and sitting alone in my apartment."

"You know, Will and I were talking…."

"Nope," Gwen interrupted, immediately recognizing her mistake. They'd had this conversation at least three times, and she wasn't interested in rehashing it.

"Come stay with us," Adrienne pressed. "You'd have your own room and bath. You wouldn't have to climb up all those stairs. Someone would be there at night if there was an emergency with the baby."

"I'm not living with you two."

"It's only temporary. Keep your apartment if you want, or let the lease expire and save up a couple months of rent to take a great trip or something when it's over. You let me stay with you when I had no place to go. Let me return the favor."

Gwen appreciated her friend's generosity, but there was no way she was going to accept the offer. "That was completely different. You were broke and homeless. I am absolutely, one hundred percent not hauling my pregnant hind end into your honeymoon bungalow."

"We've been married eight months. And a three-thousand-square-foot brownstone hardly qualifies as a bungalow."

"You're still newlyweds," Gwen said with a firm shake of her head. "Single women without elevators have babies all the time. I will be fine. Really, I'll be better off than most of them, since when it's over, I won't have a baby and all its crap to haul up and down the stairs."

"What about staying with Robert and Susan? It's their baby, after all."

"Robert and Susan live in a tiny place in Hoboken. They'd take me in, in a heartbeat, but it wouldn't be very comfortable for anyone. And I'd have a longer commute to work. No thanks."

Gwen could see the wheels turning in Adrienne's brain. Her silence made it appear as if she was backing down, but Gwen knew better.

Fortunately, the conversation was interrupted by the return of the golfing posse. The five guys strolled into the house, dumping their golf bags in the foyer and arguing loudly. Apparently there was some disagreement over Wade's handicap, the wind helping Jack cheat and whether or not it was illegal to move your ball if it fell in the cart path.

She had no real idea what they were talking about and continued to eat before her eggs got cold.

Will swept into the kitchen and wrapped his arms possessively around Adrienne, pulling her into a kiss that elicited a catcall from one of the other guys. That, precisely, was one reason Gwen wasn't going to stay with them. She wouldn't be a lumpy third wheel in their romance. And she was pretty sure she'd get depressed surrounded by all that mushy love stuff.

Alex followed Will into the kitchen and pulled a bottle of water out of the refrigerator. "Get a room," he challenged, looking at Gwen when he spoke, giving her a wide smile and winking when no one was looking.

The eggs in her mouth were suddenly dry as Styrofoam. Her cheeks were burning. Good lord. How could something as innocent as a flirtatious wink have that kind of effect on her? This man-break was going to backfire. It was supposed to help her get some perspective, but so far, all it had done was make her more vulnerable to the same type of charming man who made her want to take a break from dating in the first place.

Gwen took a big swig of her milk and stuffed a piece of cantaloupe in her mouth as a distraction. She didn't dare look up at him again.

But she did catch Adrienne watching her curiously. Her green eyes narrowed at Gwen for a moment before she turned and spoke to Alex.

"How long are you going to be back in New York this time, Alex?"

He shrugged, chugging half the bottle of water. "The project in New Orleans is under way, so I really don't need to go back down there for a while. My project manager, Tabitha, has it well under control. I was thinking of doing a little traveling this summer, though. Maybe scoping out a couple potential sites for my next project. Why do you ask?"

Yes, Gwen thought curiously. Why did Adrienne ask? And did she really want to know the answer? Probably not.

"Well," Adrienne began, "I'm worried about Gwen and that apartment of hers. It's just too many stairs, and she's all alone without air-conditioning."

"I have a window unit," Gwen grumbled.

"Like that is going to make an ounce of difference in the end of August when you're pushing eight months."

Gwen shrugged. She'd made it through the last five summers without AC. If she had to, she'd spend all her free time loitering at the ice cream place up the block from her building.

"I want her to come stay with us until the baby is born, but she's being stubborn about it."

"Are you trying to rally a gang to bully me into it?" Gwen asked, hearing the edge of her accent creeping into her voice. After five years in New York, it had mostly faded, but when she got agitated or tired, it came out in full force.

"No, actually, I had another idea. Alex's place is huge, and he's almost never there."

Gwen nearly choked on the piece of bacon she was attempting to swallow. Certainly Adrienne couldn't be suggesting that Gwen stay with Alex? As far as Adrienne knew, the two of them were casual acquaintances at best. If she knew the truth, she'd certainly keep her mouth shut on that topic.

"I know you pay some woman to water plants and collect your mail while you're away. Why couldn't Gwen stay there instead? You have that huge guest suite that no one ever uses."

Gwen's eyes widened in panic. She would not go stay with Alex whether he was there or not. It would just be weird. She turned to Alex, expecting to see him appearing equally horrified. Instead, he was just sipping his water and looking as though he were actually considering the idea. Surely a man who couldn't commit past two weeks wouldn't dream of letting a woman move in with him, even temporarily.

"I think it's a little presumptuous to invite someone to move into Alex's place without talking to him first," Will said.

Finally someone was speaking sensibly. "Especially since it's completely unnecessary." Too annoyed to continue eating, Gwen slid off her stool and planted her hands on her hips. "I am a grown woman. Y'all aren't going to railroad me into moving in with anybody. So stop wasting yer breath talkin' 'bout it."

She winced at the sound of her Tennessee roots slipping into her angry words. Before anyone could respond, she ended the conversation by spinning on her heel and dashing out of the kitchen and into her room.

Alex watched the players move back and forth across the field, but he wasn't really paying attention to the game. Normally, he liked polo. He had played for years in college, and the group they'd assembled for the charity match was like the dream team of players. But he just couldn't focus on the game. Not when thoughts of Gwen kept creeping into his mind.

He glanced to his left and saw where she was sitting with Adrienne in the VIP tent. Her bright teal dress and wide-brimmed white hat made her easy to spot in the crowd. He was glad to see she was staying out of the sun and resting for a while. The heat had been brutal today, and even though it was late afternoon, it was too hot for *him,* much less a woman in her condition.

And truth be told, he was going mad watching the beads of sweat roll into the forbidden depths of her cleavage. The plunging neckline of her dress had put her full breasts on display. She was wearing a gold-and-turquoise beaded necklace that accented the pale breadth of her skin, but it had a large teardrop medallion that rested just at the valley between the creamy orbs. He had a hard time tearing his eyes away, and eventually, someone was going to catch him.

Having her a hundred yards away and shaded from the sun removed the temptation. It also helped that Gwen had continued to keep her distance today.

After last night and the way she'd bolted after their kiss by the water, he shouldn't have been surprised. He was hoping a little time alone thinking about him would soften her resolve, but if it had, he couldn't tell. Perhaps he'd moved too fast. She hadn't minded the first time they were together, but she seemed as though she was in a different place now, mentally and emotionally. Maybe the baby had planted seeds in her mind about a family of her own. Or maybe she really was serious about this man-break thing. He could see the confusion in her eyes when he got too close. It was cloaked beneath a layer of desire, but she was obviously conflicted about getting involved with him again.

Maybe there was a reason he never returned to the same fishing hole, so to speak. Since he'd hit puberty, he hadn't spent more than a few weeks with any one woman, and not once had he seen the same woman a second time after they parted ways. Alex had convinced himself that since there were over three billion women in the world—four million of them in New York City—there was absolutely no reason for him to taste the same fruit twice.

But maybe the truth of the matter was that he knew the second bite might be sour. He knew how women thought. Even though they smiled and told you they were okay, they were lying. And when they said they weren't looking for anything serious, that just meant that you could wait a year or two before proposing. His mother had told his father something like that, then had immediately gotten pregnant so he would marry her. As far as Alex knew, they'd been miserable nearly every day since.

That would never be Alex. Unfortunately, women always wanted more than he could give, so he drew his line in the sand. One time around the block and on to the next woman before things got hairy. His methods had served him well over the years. Every romantic entanglement had an escape hatch large enough to drive his Corvette through it.

But Gwen was different.

Alex had had that thought a hundred times since he had first seen her at the welcome breakfast, and it was always about a different facet of her. She aroused him. Surprised him. Irritated him. Stirred a ridiculously protective instinct in him. And worst of all, Gwen had kept his interest. Months had gone by without him seeing her, yet she regularly plagued his dreams. The temptation of her had him breaking his own rule and rearranging his Fourth of July plans to see her again. That had never happened before.

And it was only so she could end up rejecting him. That was a new thing, too. He wasn't so pleased with how things had gone so far, but it wasn't over. He had no doubt he'd be victorious and get Gwen back into his bed.

The sound of a whistle caught his attention. The first half of the match was over. A man announced over the loudspeakers that it was time for the divot stomp and invited everyone out onto the field.

Alex watched as Gwen and Adrienne joined the others on the lawn. They laughed at each other, flipping over stray tufts of grass and looking fairly ridiculous. Gwen seemed to be having a lot of fun. He had the urge to go to her and wrap his arm around her waist to keep her steady as she hopped across the field. He wanted to hear her laughter up close. But she didn't want him there, so he held his spot, leaning against an ancient oak tree with his hands in white-knuckled fists at his sides.

Things between them had ended okay before, he thought. She hadn't asked him for more from their relationship. At the same time, she hadn't jumped at the opportunity to be with him again. Gwen was a contradiction. He didn't know where he stood with her. That alone was enough to make him want to push her and find out. That and his own burning need to possess her like the latest and greatest Apple gadget.

Alex still hadn't gotten to the bottom of what drew him to Gwen. Whatever it happened to be was as strong as ever. Strong enough to urge him to break down her walls, even though she claimed to be happy in her isolation. But what was the point, really? If he pushed her the way he wanted to, what could he give her in return? He'd tried to buy her jewelry all those months ago. He thought he'd been successful at the time, only to find out she'd relented because she'd found the perfect symbol of abstinence. That wasn't exactly what he'd had in mind.

Gwen had pushed away his physical advances. All Alex had in his arsenal was sex and money. If she wasn't interested in either, he was out of luck unless he could find another way to get her attention.

If she was after some kind of domestic existence like the one he'd very nearly dodged the day before, he couldn't help her there. But he wasn't sure she even knew what she was after. The way she'd blown hot and cold last night, he didn't know if the promise of something different between them would win her favor or send her running in the opposite direction. She'd said that she wasn't in the right place for something serious. Moments later, she wasn't receptive to something casual.

Certainly there had to be a middle ground where he could have Gwen back in his bed without grand, sweeping, romantic promises he couldn't keep. Being up-front and honest about that seemed kinder than promising what he couldn't deliver. If laughter and passion and excitement weren't enough for Gwen, then this whole week would be a waste of his time.

"Why aren't you out there stomping?" Will asked, coming up from behind him with a glass of chardonnay in each hand. He held one out and Alex gratefully accepted.

He swallowed a large gulp and let the dry bite of the wine chase away his unwelcome thoughts. "I just had these shoes polished," he said, knowing it was a lame excuse.

"Does Adrienne know you and Gwen slept together?"

Will's blunt question nearly sent a burning stream of wine up through Alex's nostrils. Instead, he fought to choke it down, swallowing and taking a painful, deep breath before he spoke. "No, she doesn't," he sputtered, and coughed into his fist. There was no sense in playing dumb. Will knew him too well and had watched him move through a line of women over the years. "Gwen doesn't want her to know."

Will nodded as he lifted his wineglass to drink. "She'd get overly romantic ideas about the two of you."

"Probably." Alex knew Will's bride was the best thing to ever happen to his friend, but she was soft-hearted and idealistic to a fault. "How did you know?"

Will glanced across the field, and Alex followed the direction of his gaze to the two women. The stomping was nearly over, and they were making their way off the field as best they could in a giggling fit. "The tension between you two is palpable. I've seen you watching her when you think no one is paying attention. When did it happen? It had to be right after the wedding."

"Yes. While you and Adrienne were on your honeymoon in Bali."

"It's been a long time since you've seen her, then."

"Yeah. You know I've been in New Orleans for months. Hell, I hadn't even spoken to her since November."

"That's certainly interesting."

Alex tried not to frown. He didn't like the implication of his friend's tone. "What do you mean by that?"

"You're still into her after all this time."

He certainly was. But he knew what Will was inferring—that perhaps he had real feelings for Gwen. He liked Gwen. He enjoyed her company. But feelings? Alex didn't have feelings about women. Not even for her.

"Why not?" he asked, dismissively. "I'd be stupid to pass up the opportunity to be with her again. She's a beautiful, uncomplicated woman who happens to be an exceptional lover. There's nothing else to it."

Will chuckled and slapped Alex on the back. "You just keep telling yourself that and maybe it will become the truth."

Alex's brow furrowed. "It *is* the truth. And besides that, she's turned me down, so there's even less than nothing to it."

Will tried to smother a smile, but failed. "Gwen turned you down? Is that an Alex Stanton first?"

He shrugged. "Maybe. But it's not over yet, so don't count me out. There's four days left to this trip. Eventually I'll convince her that I'm worth abandoning her vows of celibacy while she's here. Then she can go back to living like a nun, I'll be back on my game and Gwen will be in my past, just like all the others."

Adrienne waved at them and Will raised a hand to her. "Whatever you say, man. But if you want to keep whatever it is you two are or aren't having a secret, you'd better be more careful. I've never seen you look at a woman the way you look at Gwen. Adrienne will pick up on it in an instant." He started off across the lawn to join his wife.

"And how is that, exactly?" Alex called out to him.

Will stopped and turned, his face drawn and serious. "Almost like you wish that baby was yours."

Five

It was an exhausting day. Too much sun and noise and walking around. Too much energy spent dodging Alex's watchful gaze and Adrienne's continued arguments about her unfit living situation. By the time their parade of cars pulled into the circular driveway, Gwen was ready to sleep until her third trimester. Some of the group was talking about watching a movie, but she wasn't interested in anything but getting up close and personal with her pillow. She ignored both Adrienne and Alex's pointed looks as she excused herself and went to bed.

She resisted the urge to sleep in her clothes and managed to stay awake long enough to take off her jewelry and slip into her oversized University of Tennessee T-shirt. After that, she fell into a restless sleep pretty quickly.

Sometime after midnight, she woke up with a

miserably aching lower back. She propped a pillow between her knees and curled onto her side, but after another twenty minutes, her back still hurt and she was now wide awake.

Gwen flipped on the lamp and sat up in bed, defeated. At home, she would take a hot shower to ease her muscles, but the sight of her swimsuit on the dresser gave her a better idea. A swim in the pool would help take the pressure of the pregnancy off her body and allow her to stretch her sore muscles.

Gwen listened for noises outside her bedroom door, but it seemed that everyone had already gone to bed. Good. This would be her first time wearing her bikini since she'd gotten pregnant, and she wasn't quite ready to debut it to the world yet. She had a one-piece maternity suit that she would wear during the day with the others.

But tonight, she was free to swim as she pleased, and it would be easier to wrestle out of a wet two-piece. It was her favorite swimsuit, navy blue with tiny, white polka dots. As she slipped it on, she was pleased to find it still seemed to fit okay, although the bottoms rode lower on her hips to accommodate her belly. Gwen unlatched her bracelet, leaving it on the dresser, grabbed her towel and stepped quietly into the dark hallway. She took the direct route through the kitchen, creeping out the back door without so much as a creaking hinge.

Outside, the night was dark, but the lights of the pool were still on, giving it a shimmering turquoise glow. Wavy silver lines reflecting from the water danced along the back of the house and across the round, exposed orb of her stomach.

She tossed her towel across one of the lounge chairs and stepped to the stairs. Dipping her toe, she found the water to be cool, but not too cold. It was heated by solar panels to take the chill off. She stepped down slowly, submerging her body inch by inch until the water reached her waist. Letting go of the railing, she surged forward, cutting through the water. She resurfaced at the far end of the pool, taking a breath and pushing her wet hair back from her face.

It felt so good. Not only the water, but the weightlessness. The ache in her back immediately began to fade. She seriously needed to look into a membership somewhere with an indoor pool for the last few months of this pregnancy. Maybe a gym where she could work to get back in shape after Peanut was born. But either way, it would be worth the money, even if she just soaked in the water like a giant tea bag.

Gwen pushed off the wall and started back to the other side, stretching and pulling herself through the water. After several laps, she leaned back and let herself float at the surface. The water covered her ears and muffled the sounds around her, leaving nothing but the silent, starry night above her. She sighed, looking up at the twinkling scattershot of stars she couldn't see in the city. She hadn't realized how much she missed them until this moment.

As a teenager, she'd spent a hundred nights lying on the trampoline in the backyard doing this same thing. Watching the stars. Making wishes if one fell to Earth. Dreaming that one day she'd get out of Tennessee and do something grand and important with her life. Even at fifteen she knew she wanted to be a nurse. She wanted to help people and make a difference in someone's life.

Gwen supposed that was why she'd offered to help Robert and Susan. She'd worked for years as a nurse and had wanted to do more. Short of treating soldiers on the battlefield or children in third world countries, she wasn't sure what more she could do. But helping them have a baby was special. That would make a difference in their lives.

She let her hands drift up over her head, then brought them quickly to her sides, sending her gliding over the surface of the water. As Gwen drifted to a stop, she saw a meteor streak across the sky and dissolve into the atmosphere.

"We need to make a wish, Peanut," she said. "What shall we wish for?"

There were so many choices, Gwen had a hard time trying to decide. Of course she wanted a healthy, happy baby girl for Robert and Susan, but she didn't want to use her wish for that tonight. Every decision she made in her life was to make things better for others. Usually, knowing she'd helped someone when they'd needed it most was enough for her. But tonight, as selfish as it might seem, this wish, this star, was just for her.

But what did she want? She spent so much time worrying about other people that she didn't have a clue. Her career wasn't enough anymore. Even having a child for someone else wasn't as satisfying as she'd hoped it would be. It had been more confusing than anything. What did she want? Freedom? Family? Passion? Excitement?

"What do I want?" she said aloud to the night. Maybe the stars would point her in the right direction. As the question turned in her head, thoughts immediately drifted to Alex's bright, disarming smile. His messy hair. She could almost hear his muffled laughter through the water.

Gwen wanted to wish for Alex. She might as well wish for the moon. It would be a better use of a falling star to ask for immunity from his charms instead. Then she could get through the week without giving in to him. That seductive grin of his was nothing but trouble for a girl sworn to temporary celibacy.

"But I want him, Peanut. And I shouldn't. What should I do?"

"Personally, I'm not big on self-sacrifice, so I say if you want him, then have him."

The muffled voice made it through the water to her ears. Startled, Gwen shot upright, sinking under the surface and then bobbing back up to the top.

Wiping the water from her eyes, she saw Alex standing at the edge of the pool. He was wearing a pair of unbuttoned jeans and nothing else. The sight of his bare chest with its hard angles and defined musculature sucked the breath from her lungs. She remembered what it felt like to run her finger over the ridges and how the sprinkle of dark blond chest hair tickled her nose when she rested her head on him. Her eyes followed the trail of hair as it darkened and disappeared into his low-slung jeans. There didn't appear to be anything under them, as though he'd just tugged them on to run downstairs.

A sudden heat flushed through her body. She wanted Alex, but she certainly hadn't wanted to announce it to him. Not when she was fighting the feelings. It just gave him ammunition to use against her. How long had he been standing there? Listening to her? Watching her white belly float along the surface? Anger quickly dampened her desire. Gwen furiously splashed a handful of water at him, sending him flying back a few steps to avoid it.

"What's that for?" he asked.

"For sneaking up on me," she snapped, her legs furiously kicking to keep her petite body at the surface in the deep end of the pool. "What are you doing out here?"

"I couldn't sleep. I came down to get some water and see if there was any of Helena's pound cake left. I saw you through the kitchen window. What are you doing swimming alone in the middle of the night? Isn't that one of the basic no-no's for pool safety?"

Gwen ignored his question, swimming toward the shallow end so she could touch the bottom of the pool. Alex followed her, walking along the concrete edge in bare feet.

"My back was killing me," she said. "It woke me up, actually. I thought the pool might help. I certainly wasn't going to wake any of y'all up to babysit me while I swim."

Alex's eyes narrowed at her with concern. He seemed to be doing that a lot the last few days. She wished he'd just go back to glaring at her with poorly masked desire. That, she knew how to deal with. Sorta.

"Would you like me to rub your back for you? I give great massages."

Gwen's gaze darted to meet his. The concern was gone, the playful, seductive Alex returning. Yes, he gave good massages. She'd been treated to one in his apartment, complete with musky-scented massage oil and a happy ending for them both. His hands had been like slick magic on her skin. But that was then. Letting him try it after going months without a man's touch, even for something as innocent as a back rub, would ruin her plans. She'd fall off the wagon so fast, she'd be rolling in the dirt behind it.

Instead, she just shook her head. "That's a nice offer, but no thanks."

Alex crouched down at the edge of the pool. "You've been avoiding me since I kissed you."

Gwen opened her mouth to deny it, but there really wasn't much point. It was true. "Yes."

"Why?" His golden eyes were shrouded in the darkness, but she could still see the slightly pained expression on his face. Why her refusal would hurt him was a mystery when he could have any woman he wanted.

"Because I told you I am off men right now. You just don't listen. I'm trying to take some time for me, to organize my priorities, and I'm sorry, but you nibbling on my ear doesn't help. I don't need the distraction. It's just not a good idea."

"I don't agree. Seeing those curves of yours in that tiny bikini makes me think it's a marvelous idea. We could have a couple great days together, then you can go back to prioritizing all by your lonesome. What could it hurt?"

Gwen planted her feet on the floor of the pool and pushed herself to stand. "Me," she said, the water swirling around her stomach with the sudden motion. "It can hurt *me,* Alex. I really don't know what I'm doing anymore. This surrogacy was supposed to help me figure out what I want, but with only a few months left, I still don't know. But I'm trying to make some positive changes in my life. And, yes, I might want you. But, and I'm sorry if this offends you, I can't help thinking that getting involved with you again is a step back for me, not a step forward."

"I don't think I've ever had a woman tell me that before. Usually, I'm an upgrade." The playful glint faded from his eyes. "Gwen, you know that I—"

"—don't do relationships," she interrupted. "I know. And I was okay with that the first time. I certainly wasn't looking for anything serious." Gwen brought her hand to her stomach and stroked it beneath the water. "And I'm not looking for something serious now. I'm not looking for anything at all. But when I'm ready, I think I want something better for myself. And I don't think you're the man to give it to me."

"Gwen, I'm sorry I—" He reached out, but the wide moat of water kept her out of his grasp.

"Don't apologize, Alex. You are always up front about what you're selling. This time, I'm just not in the market to buy it."

Alex watched from the side of the pool as Gwen looked away, uncomfortably, to study one of the deck chairs. She'd spoken forcefully, putting up a brave front, probably hoping he'd just nod and go away so she didn't have to keep it up any longer. He could see she was struggling. Walking in on her private conversation had just proven to him that he was right. Gwen did want him. She was just being stubborn about it. He didn't get it. But there was only one way to get her to confess the truth. Alex would goad her into saying it.

"You're a chicken," he said.

Gwen's head snapped back toward him, her eyes wide with confusion and irritation. "What makes you think you know so much about me, Alex? I was nothing but Miss October to you."

"Maybe, but October is my favorite month, and I have an eye for details. My business wouldn't be doing as well as it is if I didn't understand people and what makes them tick. I know exactly what will capture their imagination and make them trip over themselves to buy one of my properties. And in my years with women, I've figured out quite a few additional things about them. And you."

"Like what?" she challenged.

Alex crouched down at the edge of the water to get closer to her. "Like how you never take any time for yourself. From the first moment I saw you, you've been killing yourself to make other people happy. For Adrienne's wedding. For the hospital and your patients. For your friends. Even for me during our brief time together. Now you've taken it to a whole new level, and you're having a baby for someone else."

"What's wrong with that?"

"Nothing," he argued, "unless you're suffering because of it. There's a fine line between a saint and a martyr. You don't have to be miserable to do what's important to you. It's about balance. When was the last time you did something just for you?"

Gwen frowned at him. He could see her struggling to come up with an answer, her cheeks flushing red with anger because it was taking longer than she wanted it to. "The last time I did something selfish was giving in to my fling with you."

He'd been expecting her to admit to something like splurging on a new dress or a pedicure. He never dreamed her answer would be something that had happened eight months ago. She was more caught up in this than he thought. "Why is doing something just for you selfish? The opposite of a giving person isn't a selfish one."

Gwen sighed and shook her head. "Okay, fine. You win. What do you want me to say, Alex?"

"I want you to admit that you want me."

Her jaw tightened, her dark eyes glittering with the night lights. "What does it—?"

She started to argue, but Alex cut her off. "Say it," he demanded.

"I want you," she said, but there was more irritation than passion behind her words. He wanted her to say it as though she meant it. And she would before the night was over.

Alex stood and suddenly walked off the edge of the pool, splashing into the water, jeans and all. Gwen leaped back in surprise, but she didn't have her protective moat any longer. Alex lunged at her, wrapping his arms around her waist and pulling her close.

"What are you doing?" she gasped.

"Say it like you mean it, Gwen."

Her eyes widened and she squirmed uncomfortably under his scrutinizing gaze. "It doesn't matter. I already told you I'm not interested in another fling," she argued.

"So you've said, but you're deluding yourself." He looked down and noticed the hands pressing against his chest. "You've taken your chastity bracelet off."

"The chlorine is bad for the silver," she sputtered. "It is not some subconscious invitation."

Alex smiled. She could say all she wanted, but he took it as a sign. "You and I both know there's no point in spending this whole trip denying the fantastic connection between us."

She immediately stilled, her breath catching in her throat.

"I know it would be easier if I just went back into the house and never touched you again. But I don't want to. It might be selfish, but I'm not ready to give up what we have yet. I can't stop thinking about how badly I want you, Gwen."

He didn't wait for Gwen's response. Instead, he brought a hand up to her face and cupped her cheek.

Her chocolate-brown eyes were still wide with surprise, but now a faint smile curved her full lips. That was all the invitation he needed. He leaned down to her, lifting her easily from the water that made her feel light as a feather.

When his lips touched hers, a surge of white-hot need knifed through his body, but he fought to control it. He wanted Gwen, but he didn't want to rush this. He needed to take it slowly and help her navigate her way back to trusting their sexual chemistry.

Gwen's mouth was soft and hesitant at first. She opened up to him slowly, her silky tongue gliding along his lip and teeth, teasing him. It took every ounce of restraint Alex had not to crush her against him and devour her with his mouth. Instead he let his tongue seek her out, tasting her, savoring the feel of her in his arms. She was like a rare wine. He wanted to take in her scent, let the flavor of her roll around in his mouth so he could truly appreciate it, and commit her to his memory.

His hands moved down the slick contours of her body. They glided over the cool silk of her skin, teasing him with her soft contrast to his hardness. Stepping back through the water, Alex moved them to the edge of the pool. Without his mouth leaving hers, he lifted her up to sit on the edge and erased the disadvantage of their height difference.

Gwen gasped as her backside met with the cold concrete, but she quickly recovered by opening her thighs and tugging him closer to her. The chilled pebbles of her breasts dug into his chest and echoed the heat of his arousal that pressed into her bare thigh.

Alex dipped his head to lick a drop of water that traveled down to the hollow of her throat. The sharp taste of it mingled with the salt of her skin, tempting him to run his tongue along the soft curve of her neck. She tipped her head back, her fingers lacing through his hair and urging him on.

He wanted her. Every touch, every taste, every soft cry that escaped her lips demanded that he have her. His fingers tugged at the bow of her bikini top. The blue scrap of fabric came away in his hands, and he dropped it on the concrete with a satisfying, wet thump.

Alex paused to look down at the delights he'd uncovered. The full, pale breasts that had teased him from her dress earlier in the day were on display for him at last. The creamy ivory skin was firm and flawless, the strawberry-pink tips hard and reaching out to him.

He slowly brought his palms up to each, letting her sensitive nipples graze across his rough hands in lazy circles. Gwen sighed and closed her eyes, leaning back on her hands to arch them up to him. Finally, he pressed into them, cupping each breast and letting the pad of his thumb brush the tips until Gwen whimpered. It was only then that he let himself taste them. He sucked one nipple into his mouth, then the other, teasing and tugging with his teeth and tongue until she was squirming against him and clawing gently at his back.

"Alex," she whispered, an edge of need in her voice that he'd longed to hear again after all these months without her. That was the very thing he'd wanted from her earlier.

He answered with his hand, slipping it between her thighs and stroking her through the wet fabric of her suit. He could feel the shock wave of his touch as it rocked through her body. Her hips bucked wildly against his hand, the cry escaping her lips making his erection throb painfully as it grated on the rough, wet denim of his jeans.

Pushing the suit aside, he slipped one finger inside the hot, aching entry to her body. He could feel her muscles contract around him, tightening and straining against the invasion. Slowly, he pumped into her, the pad of his thumb brushing her sensitive nub with the apex of each stroke. Gwen writhed and thrashed her feet along the surface of the water as her climax built inside her. She was a wild and passionate woman, and he'd sorely missed that while he was gone.

He watched her face with anticipation, waiting for her body to stiffen beneath him. "Say it," he whispered.

"I want you, Alex!" she cried out a second before the first wave hit.

Satisfied, he captured her mouth in a kiss. Alex swallowed the strangled cry of her orgasm, his body absorbing the violent shudders and jerks until, silent and still, Gwen collapsed beneath him.

"Now, that wasn't so hard to admit, was it?"

Gwen tried to look at him crossly, but she didn't have the energy. She was still trembling, her breath coming in short gasps, when Alex scooped her off the edge and carried her out of the pool. He stood her upright near the row of lounge chairs, reaching down to wrap the towel around her shoulders.

Once he was certain she was steady on her feet, he left her side to retrieve her bikini top and slowly made his way back. His soaked jeans hung heavily on his hips, threatening to sag to his ankles if he moved too quickly.

Alex wrapped his arm around her shoulder and guided her back to the house. He gripped his waistband to allow them to move faster through the tile kitchen, slowing once they reached the carpet that would absorb the water dripping from their bodies.

Inside her room, he shut the door behind them and

flipped the lock. When he turned back, Gwen had flung off her towel. With a bold, mischievous glint in her eye, she approached him and gave his jeans a solid tug.

As expected, they slid right down without resistance, freeing his erection to jut out to her. Gwen knelt down, letting her hot breath linger on the tip for just a moment before continuing down and helping him step out of the soggy clothing. She carried it and her swim top into the bathroom, tossing them in the sink with the bottoms she had still been wearing.

When she returned, she was completely naked. Her hair hung around her shoulders in dark, wet, blond cords. Her cheeks were still rosy from her orgasm. She stopped a few feet away from him, watching him through the damp clumps of her eyelashes. Gwen seemed almost embarrassed, although it was a little late to be shy. He'd seen her naked a dozen times and had never been disappointed.

But then, it occurred to Alex that things were different this time. The changes in her body might leave her feeling insecure. She probably wasn't as appreciative of her new curves as he was. How could she not see how beautiful she was?

Alex reached out his hand to her and pulled her toward the bed. If she couldn't see it, he'd just have to show her.

Six

Gwen let Alex guide her to the bed. He tugged back the sheets for her to slip between them, then joined her there. A chill from the pool had set in once they came into the air-conditioned house. The warmth of the blanket and Alex's body near hers felt heavenly, chasing away the gooseflesh that drew up across her skin.

The blanket also made her feel less exposed. True, her swimsuit had done little to disguise her blooming pregnancy, but somehow standing naked with Alex's eyes on her had made her extremely self-aware.

The last time they were together, she was at her all-time lowest weight after months of exercise and carb deprivation. She didn't want to look like a sausage stuffed into a pink, satin casing at the wedding. Now her body was about as different as it could be. What if it bothered him more than he thought? What if he changed his mind? It was a worry that crept into her brain without her permission. She tried to chase away the negative thoughts. Alex's desire for her was quite obvious the minute she'd tugged at his pants, and it hadn't wavered. The same firm heat pressed into her hip at that exact moment.

Gwen forced herself to relax, letting her body sink into the pillows. Alex pulled up along her side, the heat of his skin running the whole length of her body. He propped on one elbow and looked down at her. There was a softness in his expression she wasn't used to seeing. Most often there was humor or mischief or desire. The longing was still there, but it was laced with a tenderness that made her chest tight.

His fingertips brushed across her forehead to push a damp strand of hair away, then softly grazed along her jaw to her mouth. "You're so beautiful," he said.

She swallowed a denial when his thumb stroked her bottom lip and stole the words. She wanted him to kiss her again. To cover her body with his and make her forget about all her worries and anxieties, if just for tonight.

He hadn't offered her more than that. But right now, that was all she needed. Some physical contact with a man she didn't have to worry about complications with. If she had thought for a second there would be anything more to it, she wouldn't have given in. But Alex was not a guy to stick around. If she wanted more, he'd be the worst possible choice. But sex between them should be easy and gratifying. There was absolutely no reason why she should deny herself the pleasure any longer.

His mouth found hers and she opened to him once again. She relished the silky slide of his tongue, the way he could coax a low moan from the back of her throat. His lips migrated to her jaw, settling in to feast on the sensitive curve of her neck. He nipped and sucked at her skin, sending throbbing impulses through her whole body.

She was surprised how quickly she responded to him. After their encounter at the pool, she would've thought she was sated enough for one night, but she was wrong. It had simply lit a fire to dry kindling and was now building to a crackling roar of desire.

Alex's hand reached out to her beneath the blankets. His palm was a searing heat against her cool skin, blazing a trail along the curves of her body. The glide of his fingertips was electric, the sizzle warming her blood.

"Are you still cold?" he murmured against her throat.

Not when he was touching her. "No," she said, kicking at the covers.

He flung back the rest and returned to feasting on her skin. As he traveled down to her breasts, Gwen was stunned by how sensitive they'd become. Just the brush of his fingertips across her tight nipples sent a sharp throb of need to her feminine muscles, tightening them into a delicious tug of pleasure.

Alex growled low against her skin, the vibration tickling and teasing at her.

The haze of pleasure thinned for a moment when Gwen realized he was moving down her body. She tensed when his hand came to a stop resting on the swell of her stomach. Would that be too much reality for him to ignore?

Gwen held her breath; her eyes squeezed shut so she wouldn't see his reaction. It wasn't until she felt the moist heat of his kiss searing across her belly that she was able to release the air trapped in her lungs.

Alex's hand moved lower, stroking the inside of her thigh. Her muscles jumped beneath her skin with anticipation of his touch. His lips followed his fingertips, her thighs gently quivering when his warm breath brushed across her exposed core. His first taste sent a bolt of pleasure through her body that arched her back off the bed. He waited until the shock waves passed before stroking her again. Gwen held her breath, trying to swallow the cries he coaxed from her, but it was too much. He had her dancing on the edge of coming undone almost instantly.

"Alex," she whispered.

He hesitated a moment, his tongue darting out one last time before sliding back up the length of her body. Alex hovered at the entrance to her body, his golden eyes gazing deep into her own. Then he slowly entered her. She couldn't help her eyes closing as she savored the feeling she'd missed all these months with him gone.

"Damn," he groaned against her lips. The rest of his body was stone still as he hovered, buried to the hilt. His arms started shaking with the strain before he allowed himself to pull back and drive into her again.

Gwen pulled her legs up to cradle him, easily riding the waves of motion that corresponded to the swells of pleasure building inside her. She'd been so close to the edge before that it didn't take long to reach it again, but she wasn't ready to give in to it. It had been eight long months since she'd given in to her desires. Having Alex in her bed again was an unexpected fantasy she'd never thought she could indulge. This moment needed to last a lifetime in case it was their last. She wasn't about to rush to the finish line, even if every nerve in her body demanded release.

She opened her eyes, trying to memorize the lines of strain across his brow as he fought for control. Gwen wanted to remember the sound of his ragged breath and the salty taste of his skin.

It wasn't until Alex stilled that she realized he was watching her, a look of curiosity on his face. "You're thinking too much. I'm not doing a good job if you're able to focus like that."

Gwen smiled, reaching up to his face and pulling him to her lips for a kiss. "You're doing a great job," she reassured. "I'm just trying to make it last."

"The good thing about orgasms," he said with a wry grin, "is that you won't run out. You can always have another." At that, he thrust hard into her and elicited a surprised cry of pleasure from her throat. "And another."

"And another," she repeated, hooking her ankles around his hips and squeezing him until he groaned.

From then on, there were no more words. Gwen gave into the sensations, clinging to him as they drove hard toward their climax. She buried her cries in his shoulder when she came undone, the hard shudder of his own release coming soon after.

When she finally caught her breath, she looked up to find Alex hovering over her, his brow furrowed, his eyes wide with unexpected panic. "What's the matter?" Gwen asked, her voice hoarse.

His jaw dropped open in shock and he just hung there, mute, until he could gather the words. "We didn't use a condom. I forgot. I was too…" He shook his head and cursed.

Normally, Gwen would've launched into full damage-control mode. How could they forget something as crucial as that? But then she remembered she couldn't get pregnant and a good portion of the panic subsided. "That's okay," she said, brushing a strand of golden hair from his face.

"No, it isn't," he insisted. "I always wear a condom. Always."

There was a touch of alarm in his eyes that worried her. "I'm already pregnant, Alex. And it's a little late for this conversation, but I was tested for everything under the sun before the in vitro procedure. What about you?"

Her question seemed to jerk him from his thoughts. He looked down at her and nodded, clearly realizing she was right, yet still obviously concerned. "I get a full panel of testing every six months, without fail. Never so much as a false positive."

That was a relief. And at the same time a touch disturbing. How many women had he charmed into bed that he was tested so often? It was a good thing she didn't have fantasies of keeping Alex. It was an impossibility.

Fortunately, he was smart about it, so their stupidity wouldn't put both her health and the baby's in jeopardy. A nurse should know better, but apparently being in Alex's arms made her lose all her good sense.

Gwen sighed and patted his arm reassuringly. "Well, it wasn't the smartest thing, but I think it will be okay just this once." Using protection the "next time" was left unsaid. The only thing that could bring down the postorgasm buzz faster than the "oops, no condom" discussion was a clingy woman talking about the future.

Alex's jaw relaxed and he gave a short nod before leaning down to kiss her. Gwen noticed there was still a tension there, but he was trying his best to hide it. She remembered how diligent he was with birth control the last time they were together. For both of them to forget...

He eased onto his side, dropping against the mattress. His arm snaked around her and gently pulled her back to his chest.

She snuggled into him, trying not to think about the

implications of his slip and the fact that he'd positioned himself so she couldn't see his expression. He hadn't immediately rushed back to his room, so maybe she was making something out of nothing. Gwen tried to focus on just being with him, and before long, she fell asleep in the protective warmth of his arms.

It was still early morning when a beam of sunlight stretched across the bed and into Alex's face. It pulled him from the comfortable fog of sleep. His eyes fluttered open, looking around for a moment in confusion at the whitewashed furniture and blue comforter before he remembered where he was.

Gwen's bed.

Easing his head up, he saw her unruly, dark blond curls and her arm draped across his chest. She was still asleep, her breathing soft and even as she cuddled against him.

Alex needed to leave if they were going to keep last night a secret from the rest of the house. He didn't want to go. He wanted to pull up the duvet and sleep away the rest of the afternoon with her in his arms, but that was just a pipe dream. If it was daylight out, he should've returned to his room a long time ago. Will always got up early, although there was no sense in tiptoeing around him. He didn't know much about the other guests in the house, but he certainly didn't want any of them to see him dash, half-naked, to his room.

All he had were his jeans. Alex swallowed a groan when he realized they were a soaking wet heap in Gwen's bathroom sink. When he had come downstairs the night before, he was after a drink and some cake. If he'd thought for a moment he'd end up in the pool or

Gwen's bed, he would've planned accordingly. And he most certainly would've brought a condom.

The memory of the slipup slapped him in the face and made sure he was good and awake now. God, he was an idiot.

No condom. How could he forget something that important? He had never had sex without one before. He wasn't about to get snared like his father. Not once, not even one time in all these years, had he allowed himself to get so wrapped up in a woman that he could let something like that happen.

Alex wasn't quite sure why it bothered him so badly. Gwen couldn't get pregnant with his child. They both vouched for being healthy. Nothing should come back to bite either of them. What was it, then, that left him with a pool of worry in his stomach?

It was just one more thing. One more difference between Gwen and every other woman he'd ever been with. Since he'd first met her, she'd gotten through almost all of his well-fortified defenses. She probably didn't even know it, but she had. He never would've sought her out again, much less made love to her, if she hadn't gotten under his skin.

Gwen had penetrated his brain, occupying his thoughts and dreams over the last months. Making him think of nothing but having her back in his arms again. She'd pierced his physical defenses last night, getting closer to him than any other woman had. Without the barrier of latex between them, their joining had been so different. It didn't just feel different; it was almost as if it meant more than he'd ever intended.

The sound of birds chirping outside the window declared it was officially morning and distracted him from his worries. He glanced over at the nightstand and the clock sitting there. It was just after six. He definitely needed to get back to his room, jeans or no. Alex picked up Gwen's wrist and slowly eased out from beneath her. She grumbled sleepily for a moment, then curled into a ball in the warm spot he'd left behind and fell back asleep.

Alex struggled to swallow a lump in his throat as he watched her sleep. Her ash-blond hair was a tangle across the pillowcase, her pink lips still swollen from his kisses. Just the sight of her like that made his chest tighten.

Typically, the morning after was uncomfortable for him. Sunlight always brought a cold dose of reality with it. Seeing a woman sleeping or just after she'd woken up had always seemed too intimate to him. The sex... that was just sex, but the reality of a woman without her carefully crafted facade was a line he didn't like to cross. It felt like relationship territory. He preferred to leave before the veil of fantasy slipped away.

It was different with Gwen. He wasn't uncomfortable watching her like this. Not even after realizing he was playing with fire. He was overwhelmed with the urge to surprise her with breakfast in bed. He wanted to make her pancakes and kiss her maple syrup–flavored lips.

Pancakes. *What the hell was that about?* It was definitely time to go.

With a sigh, Alex ran his fingers through his messy hair and headed for the bathroom before he could do something stupid, such as cooking or tossing aside every remaining rule in his relationship book. As he suspected, his jeans were still soaked and ice cold. There was no way he could bear to slip those on against his bare skin, and he'd do nothing but drip all the way upstairs. He took the jeans and her swimsuit and moved them to hang over the bar in the shower. Hopefully they would dry better that way.

He opted to grab a towel from the rod on the wall and wrap it around his waist. Turning on the water in the sink, Alex eased down and lightly wet his hair. If he ran into anyone, he'd tell them he'd taken an early-morning dip in the pool.

Alex gave a quick glance to the bed where Gwen was silently sleeping, then crept out into the hallway. He was relieved to find the house was still dark and quiet. Six was a little early for people on vacation. When he got back to his room, he immediately slipped into the shower.

As the hot water streamed over his body and washed away her scent, his gut twisted with confusion and regret about last night. Gwen was so beautiful, so passionate. She was impossible to resist, and yet he knew he should've returned to his room instead of charging into the water and claiming her. Gwen was trying to figure out what she wanted in life. She deserved a man who would marry her and fill their home with their own children, if she decided that was what she wanted.

And that wasn't Alex.

Being here with her the last few days had roused something deep inside that wanted him to be that man for her. But that wouldn't last. Not once since hitting puberty had he had a lasting interest in a relationship. He'd seen firsthand what a hell marriage could be like. His childhood home had been a battlefield with him as one of the primary weapons. Marriage was not for him. This time, despite what he thought now, was no different. Eventually, he would feel the choking noose of commitment around his throat and he'd have to leave.

So he didn't dare offer anything he couldn't give.

He'd tempted Gwen with a few days of meaningless, mind-blowing sex, and that was all it was going to be. He wouldn't even entertain the thoughts of more in the privacy of his own mind. They were counterproductive.

By the time Alex dressed and went downstairs, Will was awake and pouring his first cup of coffee. He eyed Alex with suspicion as he settled at the breakfast bar.

"You're up early." His words were heavy with meaning as he passed a steamy mug of coffee across the counter to Alex. "Trouble sleeping?"

"Something like that," he muttered into his coffee mug, avoiding eye contact with his friend, although he knew it was pointless. Will was a newspaperman. Journalism ran in his blood. He could read between the lines and sniff out the larger story better than anyone else he'd ever met.

"What are you going to do?" Will asked softly. With his own coffee in hand, he approached the bar and leaned against it so their voices wouldn't need to carry far. Gwen's room was only feet away.

"I was thinking about going for a run," Alex answered, flatly dodging Will's real question. He was considering a jog this morning. He'd pulled on a T-shirt and jogging shorts after his shower, but it was a halfhearted effort. If he left, it would just be to escape the pull of Gwen on his thoughts. He seriously doubted even that would help at this point. She'd been the only thing on his mind since he'd decided to come on this trip.

Will shook his head but opted not to press Alex further. "Do you want company? I doubt the others will be up for a while."

"Sure, let me just absorb some of this caffeine first. What's on the agenda for today, anyway?"

"Some of us were talking about going to a couple of

wineries in the area. Several do tours and tastings this time of year."

Alex frowned, despite his general fondness for wine. "What about Emma and Gwen? Neither can drink."

Will nodded, thoughtfully sipping his coffee. "I think Emma is keen on an afternoon tanning and talking to her boyfriend on the phone. I doubt she gets five minutes of peace and solitude at home the way Pauline and George hover since the crash."

"Do you think they'll follow her to Yale?"

"No." He smiled. "But I have no doubt she'll go wild with her new freedom. Hopefully not at the expense of her grades or her reputation."

Alex grinned. They both knew Alex had had at least one semester when he'd toyed with academic probation. Economics and calculus were not nearly as interesting as playing polo and checking out the latest class of freshman girls. "What about Gwen?"

Will shrugged. "That's up to her, I suppose. She could come with us and just not drink. I think at least one of them also does olive oil and cheese tastings. And she could enjoy the tours of the gardens and vineyards."

Somehow that didn't sound like Gwen's cup of tea at all. She'd put on a brave face yesterday during the long hours of yuppie polo festivities, politely turning down the caviar and foie gras canapés and blankly staring at the horses. Following it up with a day of wine tasting was probably too much for her, especially when she couldn't benefit from getting pleasantly tipsy in the process.

Perhaps this was his chance to have some uninterrupted time with Gwen away from the others. "Maybe I'll offer to stay with her. She doesn't have a car here, so she's trapped if we all leave."

"Actually, we have the little Volvo in the garage that stays at the house. I could leave her the keys."

Alex supposed that solved the problem of Gwen's stranding, but he still didn't like the idea of her being alone all day. Emma was not likely to be good company, either. "That isn't any fun. I'll skip the wineries and take her out."

Will frowned into his coffee mug. "To do what?"

"Maybe I'll treat her to a massage."

"From you?"

"No," Alex chided. "I mean a real one at a day spa. She could get a pedicure and all that. A little feminine indulgence."

Will took a sip of his coffee, watching Alex warily. "That's very nice of you. Not exactly subtle, though."

"Can't I be nice to a pregnant woman who could use some pampering?"

"Absolutely. But don't be surprised if Adrienne smells blood in the water. And even if she doesn't get suspicious, you and I both know it's not the best idea."

"Of course it's a terrible idea," Alex agreed with a grin. It would be setting himself up for a day alone with Gwen. Sort of. It wasn't as if they'd let him in the room with her. He'd likely spend at least half the day in the waiting room reading emails on his phone. But he couldn't just walk out and leave her alone all day after the incredible night they'd spent together.

And he didn't want to, if he was honest with himself.

Maybe a day out without privacy would cool his desire for her and let him take a step back, physically, if nothing else. It might also completely implode in his face and make him feel closer to her than ever, but what was life without some risk?

Alex set down his empty mug, the caffeine finally

waking him up for the day. It was too early to make the arrangements, but he'd call as soon as he could.

"You ready for that run?"

Seven

Gwen watched curiously as everyone loaded up into a couple cars to go on what she called "the winery crawl." Even if she weren't pregnant, she would've taken a pass on this particular excursion. She was tired and really not interested in discussing vintages and bouquets. But instead of a quiet afternoon lounging and reading a book, she noticed not only Emma but also Alex beside her, waving to the cars.

"You're not going?" she asked.

Alex shook his head. "Nope."

She cast a quick glance to Emma, who had spun on her heel and whipped her phone out of her pocket before the cars had cleared the driveway. "Hey, Tommy," she said as she disappeared into the house, probably not to surface for quite some time. Gwen remembered being eighteen and completely wrapped up in a guy.

Turning back to Alex, she crossed her arms over her

chest. It hadn't been as long ago as she would like to
think. The object of her reluctant attraction was wearing
khaki pants and a plaid button-down shirt, his honey-
colored hair falling into his eyes. As always, he was
charmingly irresistible, which made her feel better for
falling off the wagon. She hadn't even bothered to put
her bracelet on this morning.

"Why?"

He moved in closer, standing only inches away to
look down at her petite, barefooted frame. "I wanted
to spend some time with you and treat you to a little
indulgence."

The combination of his words and the heat of his
body so close to her own made the words she had
planned to say far more difficult to get past her tongue.
"I hope you d-didn't pass up on the trip in the hopes
we'd indulge in wild, sexual...*escapades* all day. Not
with Emma roaming around the house."

Alex smiled and placed his large hands on her upper
arms, exposed by her spaghetti-strap sundress. The simple touch sent a surge of awareness through her body.
Memories of the night before rushed through her mind.
In an instant, her breasts tightened and her sex clenched,
making her wish she hadn't taken wild escapades off
the table so soon.

"Actually, I have a surprise for you."

Gwen looked suspiciously at him. She wasn't good
with surprises. Maybe she was just jaded, but surprises
were rarely good. At least not her mother's surprises.
Occasionally, Paw-Paw would surprise her with a trip
into town for ice cream, or Gran would make her favorite chicken and dumplings for dinner. She could only as-
sume Alex had planned a good surprise, but she couldn't
help the flutter of nerves in her stomach.

Alex was watching her with concern. "You don't want your surprise?"

"No. I mean, yes," she corrected, "I want it. I'm just a little paranoid."

"Don't be. It will be a great day, I promise. Are you ready to leave?"

"I think shoes would be a good idea, first. The term 'barefoot and pregnant' isn't supposed to be quite this literal in this day and age."

Alex smiled. "Okay. You go get some shoes. I'll tell Emma where we're going, and we'll be off. You don't want to be late for the appointment."

They walked back into the house and Gwen headed to her room. Today she was wearing another of her flowing, tropical sundresses. While appropriate for a beach holiday, she found that they were loose enough to keep her from having to wear real maternity clothes. She'd managed to get by so far with elastic waistband scrubs and loose dresses, but eventually, she knew she would have to break down and buy a few legitimate pregnancy outfits. But she certainly wasn't going to wear them around Alex. She slipped into a pair of cute brown sandals and grabbed a sweater in case she got chilled wherever they were going.

By the time she emerged, she could hear the powerful purr of the Corvette's engine in the driveway. "We'll be back soon," she called out in vain to Emma and stepped outside.

Alex was waiting beside the car, the passenger door held open for her. He'd retracted the convertible top so they could enjoy the mild weather and ocean breeze. "Your chariot awaits, milady."

"Well, thank you, sugar," Gwen said as she eased

gently into the low bucket seat. Alex closed her door and went around to climb in on his side.

"So, where are we going exactly?" she asked as they pulled out onto the highway.

"I told you, it's a surprise. But it's a good one, I promise. Just sit back, relax and go with the flow for once."

Gwen laughed and leaned back in her seat. She couldn't argue with that. Enough of her life was dictated by schedules and appointments. And while she appreciated Will and Adrienne's efforts to make sure everyone had a great trip, there was something to be said for relaxing on vacation and taking a day as it comes. "All right. You win. I am at your mercy."

She closed her eyes and took a soothing, deep breath. Driving through the countryside with the top down was a rare treat. She barely rode in cars at all anymore, and there was nothing soothing about a cab ride through midtown. Riding in Alex's convertible reminded her of sitting in the back of her grandpa's pickup truck with the hay-scented wind whipping her hair around her face.

When she opened her eyes again, she could tell they were getting close to a town. There were more houses near the street and sidewalks lining the road. The Hamptons had its share of outrageous mansions, but her favorites were the quaint little cottages. Old whitewashed wood siding, covered porches, wild English-style gardens... These were here long before the ultrarich came and dotted the countryside with multimillion-dollar castles.

The houses eventually turned into shops, and she spied a sign for East Hampton. They drove past a gourmet grocer, a wine specialty store, a bakery and a neat little jewelry boutique. On the corner was a bistro with striped awnings and a shaded outdoor seating area with wrought-iron furniture. People were out and about, but it wasn't nearly as crowded and high-energy as yesterday's polo tournament. *Quaint* wasn't even the word for this place.

She kept waiting for him to stop and force her into a store. Alex had taken her shopping the last time they were together. He'd ushered her into Tiffany and insisted she choose something. It had felt ridiculous looking at cases filled with jewelry that cost more than a few months of her salary. And for what? It seemed a little excessive for a two-week tumble. The charm bracelet had been a choice to get him off her back. And she did love it. Actually, her wrist felt naked today without it, but she decided between the pool, the beach and the sunscreen it was best to leave it off. Besides, she couldn't wear her chastity bracelet while she was being quite unchaste.

Alex had been annoyed with her selection, especially when he'd found out what it symbolized for her. Perhaps he was trying again.

After driving for a few minutes, Alex pulled into a spot along the street and killed the engine. "We're here."

Gwen looked around in confusion. They were parked near the post office. That wasn't much of a surprise.

Alex climbed from the car and came around to open her door. She turned and swung her legs out, but her shifting center of gravity and the road-hugging chassis made it more challenging to stand than she'd expected. "This is definitely not a third-trimester car."

Alex stepped off the curb and offered two strong hands to hoist her out of the seat. His help made it much easier, and she was standing in an instant. A little too easy, actually, as the momentum sent her up and colliding against his chest. She clung to him to keep from bouncing back and falling. His hands slipped under her arms to cup her elbows and steady her and then slid up the backs of her arms to keep her held close against him.

Gwen looked up at him and swallowed hard. His golden eyes were focused intently on her. The light breeze was fluttering the honey layers of his hair. She reached up and brushed some out of his face, tucking them behind his ear, then left her palm resting against his cheek. It was still smooth from his morning shave, unlike last night when the rough stubble had tickled and tormented her bare skin.

Leaning down, he kissed her. It was a soft, gentle kiss. She could feel the tension building beneath his tight skin, but he held back. The middle of town, surrounded by people, was hardly the place to let his passion come unleashed. And yet Gwen couldn't help responding to him. She climbed onto her toes to get closer, their mouths and tongues meeting in an easy, comfortable dance.

It was amazing how quickly they had gotten to know each other's needs and wants. Last night, even after months apart, Alex remembered just how to touch her. Just how to elicit the response he sought. And now, standing in the middle of the quaint town, kissing outside the post office felt so natural. It was more like…a relationship kind of embrace.

If that unnerving thought didn't urge Gwen to pull away, Peanut's sharp kick to her rounded belly surely did. Alex yanked back in surprise, looking down at the stomach that had been pressed against him a moment before.

"What was that?" he asked.

Another hard thump followed. Gwen winced and gently rubbed the spot of the latest attack. "That was

Peanut. She's trying out for the U.S. women's national soccer team."

Gwen snatched one of his hands and pressed the palm firmly against the side of her tummy. Peanut didn't disappoint, throwing a hard kick to protest the pressing of her little baby cocoon.

Alex's eyes were wide with surprise when he looked at her belly, then back at Gwen. "Does that hurt?"

"Sometimes." She shrugged. "At first there was just this flutter. Then, a few weeks ago, she got strong enough to really make her presence known. Before long, she'll be beating the hell out of me."

"Why?"

"She's stretching and testing out her little muscles. As she gets bigger, I think it's harder for her to get comfortable. I know exactly how she feels. So…" she said, pulling away to give herself some breathing room. "Where's this surprise of yours?"

"Right this way." Alex took her by the hand and led her across the street to a two-story building with the sign Heaven-Leigh Day Spa hanging over the door.

A spa. A bubble of excitement formed in her chest at the thought. Gwen had to admit that, even if he just took her inside to buy her some overpriced shampoo, it would be a welcome indulgence. Anything more would be, well, *heaven-leigh*.

She paused when she noticed the sign on the door said it was closed. The bubble burst. So much for that. "Looks like they're closed."

"Looks can be deceiving." Alex ignored the sign, opening the door, which chimed gently, and ushering her inside.

A tall, willowy woman in white appeared from another room and approached the reception desk where they were waiting. "Good morning. I'm Leigh, the owner. You must be Miss Wright."

Gwen smiled. "Yes. Call me Gwen, please."

"Excellent. We have a full afternoon of pampering scheduled for you, Gwen."

Gwen turned to Alex in surprise. "A full afternoon?"

Alex just smiled and shrugged. "What else do you have to do today?"

"But the sign said you're closed."

"Yes," Leigh continued. "Mr. Stanton has reserved the entire spa for the day so we can give you our full, undivided attention. We have everything ready, including a prenatal massage guaranteed to make you feel like a million dollars. Are you ready to get started?"

She could hardly believe what she was hearing. An entire day spa reserved just for her. It was absolute insanity. And she was going to enjoy every minute of it. "Honey, you have no idea how ready I am."

Gwen gave Alex a quick kiss of appreciation, a wide grin of excitement lighting her face, and then she disappeared into the back for her day of pampering.

For the next few hours, Alex sat quietly in the Zen Lounge checking email and reading a travel magazine. Occasionally, Leigh would march Gwen through from one treatment room to the next. Each time, Gwen was snuggled contently into her bathrobe and looked as though she had fewer and fewer bones left in her body. He was glad. That was the whole point. He wanted to take care of the caretaker for once. A massage, salt glow, facial, manicure and pedicure were a good way to start.

She didn't care much for jewelry or flowers. She wasn't the kind to be impressed by the flash that drew other women. He didn't even recall her mentioning his money in any conversation they'd ever had. Usually it would come up. As the sole heir of a family fortune rivaling Rockefeller and Carnegie, there was always a curiosity about how much he was actually worth. Gwen honestly didn't care.

It was another reason he liked her. Another reason that set her apart from the pack.

But he knew this would be the thing that really excited Gwen. She deserved every minute of it. He would have spent three times the money he'd paid for today to see that relaxed, contented smile on her face.

When they were finally done with her, Gwen emerged from the ladies' changing room dressed, but still decidedly invertebrate. He offered her the choice of going home for a nap or having a late lunch at the bistro they'd seen earlier. She chose the bistro.

They walked through town toward the restaurant, window-shopping and taking in the sights as they went along. Neither of them were in a hurry, just enjoying their afternoon together. When they arrived at the bistro, they selected a table outside. Gwen sipped pomegranate tea in the shade, and she and Alex shared a brick-oven pizza with crispy prosciutto, figs, arugula and fat slices of homemade mozzarella.

After taking one last bite, Alex watched in amusement as Gwen leaned back in her chair and stroked her full belly. The dress had camouflaged her pregnancy most of the day, but the press of her hand against the fabric made it more obvious to anyone looking on. She looked beautiful sitting there with a smile of contentment on her face.

Actually, he wasn't sure if he'd ever seen Gwen look happier, and he was glad that he was partially responsible for it. There was a part of him that needed to make her smile. His father had always made a point of giving him anything he ever wanted growing up. That was just how he related to his son. When Alex was older, he did the same, giving expensive gifts to women instead of real affection.

With Gwen, giving her gifts was not enough. He wanted to see the joy in her eyes, not just the excitement of greed that other women had. It was important to him in a way he didn't understand and didn't want to really consider.

Glancing away, he noticed a group of older women coming down the sidewalk toward them. They'd been shopping, as evidenced by the variety of bags in their hands. One of the women, a slight little lady about Gwen's size, was watching them with the twinkle of an excited grandmother in her eye. He wasn't surprised when she stopped and leaned over to Gwen.

"How far along are you, dear?"

Gwen smiled. "Five and a half months."

"My youngest daughter is six months along. It's going to be my first granddaughter." She held up a bag slightly overflowing with what looked like pink fabric and lace. "Five grandsons so far, so I'm very excited. Do you know what you're having?"

"It's a girl."

"Little girls everywhere! How wonderful. I apologize for interrupting your lunch, but you're just glowing, and I couldn't help but stop. With such beautiful parents, I have no doubt that baby is going to be a little heartbreaker. You'd better watch out, Daddy."

Alex smiled appropriately and waved as the lady joined her group and continued down the street. Explaining the reality of their complicated situation to a little old lady on the street was unnecessary. And she was right.... They would have very attractive kids. With his golden hair and her curls. Gwen's dark eyes and his smile. It wasn't hard to picture a little boy and girl running around playing in the grass of their front yard.

When he turned back to Gwen, she was pensively stroking her stomach and staring off down the street. There was a slight frown on her face that snapped him back to reality. While he was daydreaming about blond children playing in a yard they didn't have, she seemed to have taken her thoughts down a darker path. One that focused on the fact that the baby wasn't theirs and the "daddy" was just her on-and-off, commitment-phobic lover.

That made him frown, too. What the hell was he thinking even entertaining the idea of what their children would look like? That was the kind of fantasy a smitten teenage girl would concoct while thinking about her crush. He was a grown man. One determined never to even have children. What was it about Gwen that made him think such bizarre, unproductive things?

Alex shook his head irritably and threw enough cash on the table to cover their check. "Are you ready to go?"

Gwen turned back to him, snapping out of her thoughts and nodding. The frown was gone, but he could still see the worry puckering her eyebrows beneath her sunglasses.

He wanted to say something, but he wasn't quite sure what. With the precariousness of their relationship, many things could be interpreted wrong. There were still a few days left of the trip. Saying the wrong thing now could make the rest painful at best.

Alex reached out his hand to help her from her chair. "She was right about one thing. You are glowing," he said once she got to her feet.

Gwen searched his face for a moment, then shook her head dismissively. "Of course I glow. I just had a very expensive and thorough facial and sea salt scrub."

"True, but you've had a rosy, maternal radiance this whole time. Today's treatments only made you relax." He leaned down and placed a kiss against her exposed shoulder. "And even more silky soft, if that's possible."

He took Gwen's hand and led her through the tables to the sidewalk. They walked silently back to the car and didn't speak during the drive to the house. When Alex turned into the driveway, he noticed the other cars had returned. He stopped the convertible, not wanting to end his wonderful day with Gwen on such a somber note.

"What are you doing?" she asked.

Alex shifted the car into Neutral, engaged the parking brake and turned in his seat to face her. "I hope you had a good time today."

Her dark eyes widened for a moment before the corner of her mouth turned up just slightly. She looked down into her lap as though she were embarrassed. "I did. You don't know how badly I needed a little TLC. Thank you, Alex. It was very thoughtful of you."

"You don't seem very happy now. Did that woman at the restaurant upset you?"

"No," she said. "She just made me think about things I've been trying to ignore."

"Like what?"

"Like what life is going to be like after the baby is born. After this vacation ends and you're gone again. In that woman's mind, I was just starting out on the wonderful adventure of parenthood with you by my side. The truth is that in four months, I'm going to be alone with nothing to show for the last year of my life but some oversized clothes."

Alex didn't know what to say. He wouldn't insult her intelligence by attempting to comfort her with the empty promise of his staying. The baby wasn't hers to keep. Her worries about him and what he could offer were valid. So he didn't say anything. Instead, he leaned over and wrapped his arms around Gwen, pulling her to his chest.

There was no heat in his touch. Only comfort. She accepted it, snuggling against him and burrowing her face into his neck. They sat that way for several minutes. He could feel a cool dampness sinking into the cotton of his shirt and realized she was silently crying. He didn't say anything, just held her tighter and waited for the tears to dry.

At last, Gwen spoke, her voice almost too quiet for him to hear it. "Come to my bed again, tonight."

He nodded against her, brushing a bit of her hair back to press a kiss to her forehead. "I will."

Eight

The following day included a group excursion to the beach. Their stretch of harbor property was a little too rocky, so they loaded up the Land Rover with chairs, umbrellas and coolers and left midmorning in their usual caravan of cars.

Adrienne pointed out an empty stretch of white, sandy beach, and they pulled the cars off the road to claim it. With so many people, it didn't take long to get everything unloaded. Gwen tried to help, but Alex just frowned at her and insisted she make herself comfortable in the lounge chair he'd set up for her. She didn't argue, carrying her bag over and settling in to stay out of everyone's way.

Will and Alex set up a large umbrella just behind her to shade a couple of the chairs. Except for Helena, who had a dark, Italian glow to her skin, the other women were all extremely fair and would burn even with sun-block.

As the others unpacked and set up, Alex brought Gwen a bottle of citrus-infused water and a can of SPF 75 sunscreen spray. "Be sure to drink as much water as you can and keep plenty of this on today. It's hot, and I don't want you getting dehydrated."

He had been fawning over her since they got home yesterday. Almost like a man would pamper his expectant wife. Crying in his arms had probably been a bad idea. It felt good to get it out of her system, but now he probably thought she was both emotionally and physically fragile. He'd even handled her a bit more delicately in bed last night. It was wonderfully passionate and romantic, yet she didn't remember Alex being a particularly tender lover before.

Gwen took the water and the sunscreen from him and noticed Adrienne watching them as she unpacked a few beach towels from a tote bag. "Stop fussing. It's not exactly subtle," she said.

Alex shrugged. "I'm more worried about the welfare of you and the baby than anything else, including being found out by the relationship police."

For a brief moment, the expression on his face was serious and concerned. No smirks, no winks, no grins. He was honestly worried about her. She wasn't quite sure how to respond, especially when the charming smile returned and he wandered off to help Wade and Jack unpack a few bagged chairs. He was so confusing.

After the last few days, her confusion was only getting worse. Alex was the fun guy, the exciting guy. Not the caring, relationship guy. And yet, since they'd been in the Hamptons together, that was almost how it had felt. The wild, passionate nights were paired with conscientious and thoughtful days. If Alex was any other man, Gwen might start to wonder if something more was going on between them.

But tigers didn't change their stripes.

Instead of worrying too much about something she couldn't control, she decided to do as he'd said and start rubbing in sunscreen. She could already feel the warmth on her skin that was a certain precursor to burning. Fortunately, today she'd opted for her one-piece suit so less skin was exposed. It was black and purple, and she tied a multicolored sarong low on her hips. After applying the lotion to every inch she could reach, she set the can aside and eased back into her chair with the water he'd brought her. Now that she was protected from burning, it was easier to relax and let the heat sink into her bones.

She'd spent another wonderful night with Alex. Combined with yesterday's massage, there were parts of her body she didn't even know could hurt, but she couldn't regret it. Being with Alex was a welcome distraction from reality. This trip, this place, this romance... It was all a fantastic dream she would wake up from the moment Will's car crossed back into Manhattan.

She'd tried not to let yesterday linger on her mind. She and Alex had had such a good time walking around and having lunch. His spa surprise had been a spot-on choice. She couldn't think of a single thing he could've bought her that she wanted or needed more. He really did seem to have her figured out. Or maybe he just understood women in general. What woman wouldn't appreciate a day at the spa?

Gwen had thoroughly enjoyed the tiny glimpse into what life could be like together. The sweet lady's comments at the bistro had simply snapped her out of the romantic reverie she'd drifted into. It wasn't her fault that in that moment, Gwen wanted so badly for it to be real. That they were a loving husband and wife vacationing. Expecting their first child together.

It had taken a while for Gwen to admit to herself that was part of her problem. She was falling for this fantasy they had going. It had lulled her into the idea that having a husband and family was something she wanted—something she *had.* Gwen's hand went to her stomach, stroking the curve through the stretchy black fabric of her suit. But she didn't have anything. It was not her baby. It was not his baby. She needed to keep telling herself that.

She couldn't help but glance up to where the guys were now playing Frisbee in the sand. Alex was wearing only a pair of fire-engine red swim trunks. He moved quickly, snatching the disk from the air and immediately firing it off in Wade's direction. She admired the athleticism and grace of Alex's movements as his strong muscles flexed beneath his tanned skin.

He was not hers, either. Gwen sighed and took a sip of her water.

Gwen had been thinking the strangest things over the last few days. She wasn't sure if it was the baby, being around happy married couples, hormones, or having Alex's warm presence in her bed at night, but it made her want more. For the last eight months, she hadn't been able to target what she really needed in her life. Maybe it was because she'd labeled the thing she needed the most with her mother's ugly stigma and couldn't see past it.

Love and marriage and family.

If that was what she wanted, certainly she could do it differently, right? It was such a huge leap for her, to want the one thing she'd always told herself she didn't need. But she wanted to try. If it didn't work, she could always go back to the way she'd done things before.

If she was going to start entertaining the idea of marriage and family, okay. Gwen was more open to that than she'd ever been before. But to have it, she needed to start with the basics—a man who loved her and wanted to marry her.

Yes, and all she needed to buy her own tropical island was a couple million dollars. Easy fix, right?

Gwen turned to watch Adrienne spread out a beach towel on the chair beside her and settle in with her own drink and a paperback to read. She looked adorable in her hot-pink bikini, her dark brown hair swept into a ponytail. There was no need for her to cover any of her curves with a wrap like Gwen had. She set her items on top of the small cooler that separated them and started applying sunblock to her legs.

"I thought you'd sworn off men," Adrienne said casually, slathering on the thick white cream.

"What?" Gwen looked up and followed Adrienne's line of sight to Alex. "Oh."

"When were you planning on telling me?"

Gwen gave a quick glance around to make sure no one else was within earshot. For now the coast was clear. "How did you find me out? Was it the fussing? I saw you watching us."

"Not really. That was just the latest of a hundred clues. You two are both ignorant if you think that kind of sexual attraction can be disguised. Even a ten-thousand-square-foot house on three acres is too small for people not to notice something is going on. So... Tell me what's going on."

Gwen shrugged dismissively. "Not much to tell really."

Adrienne turned to her, a curious arch to her eyebrow. "I find that hard to believe."

Her best friend was too intuitive for her own good. But short of the torture of thumbscrews, Gwen wasn't going to admit to anything more than a fun fling. After all, that was all they'd agreed to. All that it was supposed to be, regardless of how it might feel. "I'm sorry to disappoint. But you know Alex and his track record with women well enough to realize there isn't going to be more to this story than some good sex."

"Good?"

"Okay," Gwen admitted with a sly grin. "*Great* sex. He has most certainly earned his reputation with the ladies."

Adrienne smiled and started smearing the sunblock into her arms and shoulders. "How long has this great sex been going on?"

"Two days. If you don't count the two weeks after your wedding." She said the last sentence quickly, following it with a swig of water from her bottle as if she could slip the shocking news past her friend. From the look on Adrienne's face, it didn't work.

"So, what…eight months?"

"No. Eight months sounds like it's something. Eight months with a nearly seven-and-a-half-month gap in between is clearly nothing."

"But you've kept it a secret from me for that long. If it was nothing, you could've told me."

"I know." Gwen winced at the admission. "But I knew you would get spun up about it. If something went wrong, it would make things awkward, with us being friends with you and Will. It was just easier this way. I don't want this made into any more than it is."

"Great sex," Adrienne said flatly.

"Yes. I have to say I hadn't come up here intending on picking up anything with Alex. I turned him down several times. But a combination of pregnancy hormones and that damned seductive smile of his changed my agenda pretty quickly."

Adrienne nodded sympathetically. "Alex's charm is hard to ignore."

Gwen looked back out toward the water. Sabine and Emma had waded out into the waves with boogie boards. The guys were still playing Frisbee. As though he could feel her eyes on him, Alex turned to Gwen and shot her a smile before turning back to the game.

"Indeed," she agreed. Every nerve in her body had responded to him in that instant. Even after a long night of thoroughly exhausting lovemaking, she wanted more of him. And not just his body.

It was a dangerous thought, because that was all Alex could offer her. At best, she would walk away from this week with some fond memories and a fabulous day at the spa. If she let herself get too involved in this fantasy, she would walk away with a bad case of heartache. Either way, one thing she wouldn't have come next week was Alex.

Frowning, Gwen quickly scrambled into her bag for a magazine she'd brought with her. She needed a distraction. Anything to keep her brain from the train of thought it was determined to take. She'd just told Adrienne this was nothing and now, seconds later, she was sitting here thinking the exact opposite.

Flipping open the magazine, she thumbed through a few pages until she found an article on something completely unrelated to sex or love.

"Just do me a favor, though."

Adrienne's words pulled Gwen from the details of this fall's hot hairstyle trends. "What's that?"

"I know that you're not really into the long-term thing, so it might be a moot point. But don't let yourself fall in love with Alex. I've only known him a few years, but it doesn't take long to realize that behind the charm and the money is a man running from something. Plenty of women have wasted time and energy trying to chase after him only to find themselves empty-handed. I'd hate for you to be one of them."

"Of course," Gwen said, turning back to her magazine with a forced smile on her face. "I'm not stupid."

But inside, she knew the truth. If she wasn't careful, she would be on track to becoming the stupidest woman on the planet.

Alex clutched his drink in one hand and the deck railing of the ship with the other as his stomach lurched. He hated boats. Dinghies, canoes, yachts, cruise liners… It didn't matter. Even the most expensive stabilization systems and motion sickness pills couldn't keep him from getting nauseated. It was ironic, really, since his family owned a multimillion-dollar yacht and he hadn't set foot on it even once in the ten years since his parents bought it.

This boat was harder to circumvent. Will and Adrienne had chartered a dinner yacht to cruise out into the water at sunset. There was no avoiding it, especially when he saw the light of excitement in Gwen's eyes when she found out about their plans. It was a lovely, romantic idea in theory. He popped a couple Dramamine and hoped he could keep the meal down. Throwing up over the side of the railing was a definite mood killer.

So far, so good. Dinner had been an excellent New

England clambake-style spread. He could forget where he was while gorging himself on perfectly cooked seafood and spicy seasoned vegetables. Fortunately, the wind had died down. The water was relatively calm, with the reflection of the full moon dancing across it. But every now and then, they'd hit a larger wave and he'd seriously regret the chocolate lava cake they'd had for dessert.

After dinner, the ship was set to cruise around for an hour with a fireworks display before returning to the pier. The deck was decorated with colored lights and music was piped out through speakers all over the ship. Everyone seemed to be happy to talk and laugh, sipping their drinks and watching the lights from the shore twinkle in the distance. It really was a perfect night to be out sailing. If you liked that sort of thing.

Alex had quietly asked the bartender for some ginger ale in a lowball glass and moved away from the crowd not long after dessert. He found a quiet corner of the ship where he could take a moment to breathe deeply and let his dinner settle. If anything went awry, there would be no witnesses. No one knew about his issue with boats, and he preferred it to stay that way.

The wind picked up, ruffling his hair, and before he knew it, the up-and-down movement of the boat went from almost tolerable to gut-wrenching. His stomach churned and he broke out in a cold sweat.

"You've been holding that same drink for an hour," Gwen said, coming up to him.

Damn. It was bad enough to feel sick, but he certainly didn't want to be sick around Gwen. "I'm not feeling much like drinking tonight. Too much sun at the beach, I think."

Gwen watched him curiously for a moment, her eyes narrowing. "You look a little green."

"I'm fine."

"Alex, I'm a nurse, remember? You can't fool me. Are you feeling seasick?"

He gritted his teeth and gave a curt nod. Before he could say anything else, the ship rocked and the battle was over. Alex ran around the corner out of her sight and hung over the back of the ship to return his dinner to the sea. When there was nothing left, he rinsed his mouth out with ginger ale and spit it out. Feeling a hundred times better, he closed his eyes and slumped over to rest his forehead on the white metal rails.

Gwen didn't speak, but he knew by her scent the instant she sidled up beside him. Something soft and cold pressed against the back of his neck. "This wet towel should help," she said. "And suck on one of these."

Alex opened his eyes to see one of her peppermint candies in her hand. He unwrapped it and put it in his mouth. The mint was surprisingly soothing to his upset stomach. It wasn't long before he started feeling normal again.

"Feeling any better?" she asked.

"Yes. You're an excellent nurse." He attempted a grin, but his heart just wasn't in it.

Gwen gently rubbed his shoulder, then turned to grip the railing and look out into the water. "The moon is beautiful tonight."

Alex looked at her, the moonlight making the pale skin of her face glow against the dark tangle of curls that hung loose around her shoulders. Her dark burgundy satin dress was sexy and short, tying just above the waist, accentuating the swell of her pregnancy and leaving her nicely shaped calves gloriously bare. She was wearing low heels tonight so the daring, V-cut neck-line of her dress brought the soft curves of her breasts a touch closer to tempt him. "You look beautiful to-night, too."

"Thank you," she said, her nose wrinkling as though she was uncomfortable with the compliment.

Alex never understood why women were always hes-itant to accept compliments. Despite accusations that he was a ruthless charmer, he didn't hand them out lightly. He always meant what he said. He was a lover of women. Seeing them smile, hearing them laugh, watch-ing them blush... He did whatever it took to coax their best from them. If that made him a charmer, it made other men lazy.

"Do you need another drink? Some club soda, maybe?"

Alex shook his head. "I already have ginger ale, thank you. Besides, you following me back here and fetching me drinks won't look good. You called me on being too obvious this morning. How subtle is the two of us disappearing to be alone on the ship?"

"It doesn't matter. We've been outed."

"Adrienne?"

She nodded. "Apparently neither of us has a future as a ninja or spy."

"So much for my retirement plans." Alex pulled the towel from his neck and tossed it into a bucket on the deck. He leaned his forearms onto the railing, bring-ing his height more in line with hers. "She have much to say about it?"

"Not as much as I expected, but she put in her two cents. Mainly, she advised me not to fall in love with you."

"That's wise," he agreed. "It's hard to be in love with someone who isn't into relationships."

There was a short hesitation before Gwen responded. "Is that really true?" she challenged. "That you aren't 'into' relationships? Or is it just a convenient excuse?"

Alex frowned and snorted dismissively. "And what exactly is your diagnosis, Nurse Wright?"

"It's hard to say, since I don't know much about how you were raised or what experiences you've had, good or bad. Adrienne said she gets the feeling you're running from something, and I agree. Intimacy, maybe? You've just decided you'd rather act like you're too cool to settle down, when the truth is you're trying to avoid the pain of a failed relationship."

"That's a very bold guess for someone who admits they know nothing about me."

"It feels true. You do everything you can to avoid letting a woman become important. Short or onetime encounters, buying expensive but meaningless gifts, traveling all the time, moving from one woman to the next... It just makes me wonder."

"Wonder what?"

"It makes me wonder who hurt you so badly that you refuse to even take the chance on something great happening."

Alex tried without success to swallow the lump that formed in his throat and took a sip of his drink to see if it would help. It didn't. He had never realized he was that transparent. Maybe it was only obvious to Gwen. She saw things other people didn't bother to notice. She'd just said something to him that no one else in his entire life had had the nerve or interest to ask. She was nothing if not honest, direct and sincere. He supposed she deserved the same. "I don't believe in love."

Gwen turned to him and gave a soft nod of understanding. "Sometimes, I'm not sure I do, either. What convinced you?"

"Because I've never seen it last longer than the hormone surge. By the time that wears off, odds are you've done something stupid like get married or pregnant and now you're stuck with someone you find you don't even like."

"Like your parents?"

A smile curved the corner of Alex's mouth. She was an insightful little minx. "Well, they *are* a child's closest example of how relationships work. Mine taught me they don't. They've always been miserable together, but they keep up the ruse for appearances' sake. They're rarely in the same room together. My father escaped into his work. I almost never saw him growing up, and when I did, he was buying me something. My mother used me to get what she thought she wanted, then blamed me my whole life when it backfired on her. They smile for the cameras on family holidays, but that's about it. Doesn't exactly make you want to run out and get married, does it?"

Gwen shook her head. "My parents never married. My father split before my mother was even as pregnant as I am right now. She's spent every moment since then trying to catch and keep a man. Her quest was the most important thing in her life. Even more important than her only child. Her priorities are so messed up. It just makes me more determined not to be like her. I tend to fall for the kind of guys who aren't going to stick around, so I don't bother with getting attached."

"And to think, I thought you liked me for my smile."

Gwen gave him a watery grin and turned back to focus on the ocean. "But lately I wonder if I'm missing out on something. It's like I'm the only kid in school who doesn't believe in Santa, so I'm not getting any presents. Maybe for Peanut's sake, I want to believe. I want love and happy marriages to exist because I want it for her. Is that weird?"

"No. People want better for their kids than they had. At least, they should. The problem is when people have children for the wrong reasons. Although my mother would never admit to it, my father told me when I was grown that she deliberately got pregnant with me so he would marry her. That certainly worked out well for her." Alex couldn't keep the bitter sarcasm from slipping into his voice.

"Are you worried someone would try to do that to you? Trap you with a child? I could imagine that would be a good reason to be such a condom fanatic."

Alex had been called a great many things in his life, but that was a first. "I suppose you could say that. I know it's hard for people to understand, but when your estimated worth is plastered across the pages of different newspapers and magazines, you're naturally a target. Of competitors, swindlers and gold diggers alike. I don't trust a woman to be genuine with me. They all want something from me. Except, maybe you."

Gwen turned to him with a confused look that drew her delicate eyebrows together. "I'm not sure if I should be flattered or not."

"Be flattered. It puts you above millions of other women in New York." Alex paused and listened for a moment to the music playing on the deck. "Do you hear that? They're playing our song."

Gwen wrinkled her nose. "We have a song?"

"I'm insulted," he said, pushing away from the

railing and sweeping her into his arms. "This is the song we danced to at the reception."

Alex didn't make any fancy moves to keep the seasickness from returning but held Gwen against him and gently circled around their private section of the deck. She swayed easily and comfortably in his arms to the slow, sultry music. He thought for a moment she might let their conversation lapse, then he heard her speak quietly into his lapel.

"So, is it that you don't believe in love, period, or you don't believe anyone will ever love you for who you are?"

Alex shrugged. "What does it matter? I can't change who I am. So whether it exists or not, that means no love or family for me."

"You don't want children at all, then?"

There was a touch of disappointment lining her eyes when she asked the question. It didn't surprise Alex. Gwen told him she didn't believe in love and marriage, but even since they'd been here, he'd noticed a change in her. There was a touch of sadness in her eyes when she watched Will and Adrienne together. The same sadness that was there after the woman had confused them for a married couple.

She wanted it. And not just for Peanut. Judging by the way she was looking at him, part of her entertained the idea of having it with him someday. The fair-haired babies of yesterday's fantasy popped back into his mind. Surprisingly, he'd been guilty of those thoughts as well.

Alex sighed. "It's not that, so much. The idea of having children by choice doesn't bother me. I just don't think children should be brought into a marriage without love. And I don't believe in love, or marriage, so kids are automatically out of the question."

"I suppose that's why you almost choked on your tongue when you saw me pregnant."

"Not exactly."

Gwen frowned at his response. "What does that mean?"

Alex swore he'd never voice these words out loud, but something urged him to get it off his chest. Maybe saying them would send them out to dissipate in the atmosphere instead of locking them inside to slowly poison him. "It was the opposite, really. I mean, there was this wild mix of surprise, fear and anger because I thought you'd kept it from me. But there was also a part of me..."

Gwen leaned into him, her dark eyes widening in anticipation of his words. "Yes?"

Her eagerness gave him pause. Telling Gwen how he really felt would just open the door to an opportunity that wasn't real. Even though the idea of fatherhood had intrigued him, it was a gut reaction. His ancient, caveman biology taking over. He thought better of it now. He would never marry or have children, and he hadn't changed his mind about that.

Raising her expectations was unfair. Really, everything he'd said or done to her since he'd come to the Hamptons was unfair. He should've walked away from the pool and not dragged her back into whatever it was they shared. Alex needed to put the brakes on this whole thing before he did any more damage.

A loud pop sounded in the distance and they both turned to see a shower of white sparks fall into the sea. It was followed by a burst of red, then green. The fireworks display had begun, lighting the sky and the water surrounding them with bright, colorful explosions. It was a beautiful and welcome distraction.

He watched them for a moment, then shook his head.

"Adrienne was right," he said, taking a step back from her and ending the dance. "Don't let yourself fall in love with me, Gwen."

At that, he turned and disappeared around the corner to rejoin the others.

Nine

Gwen waited almost an hour in her room that night before she realized Alex wasn't coming. She'd made the mistake of thinking that their conversation was a step forward. He was opening up, sharing his past and his feelings. But then he'd walked away and she hadn't spoken to him in the hours since then. The empty space in the bed beside her only confirmed how wrong she was. Alex hadn't just walked away from the uncomfortable conversation; he'd walked away from her.

She wasn't quite sure what was going on with him, but she could see through his suave, womanizing veneer now. He obviously chose not to let anyone, especially women, get close to him. He had his reasons. She understood that much, because she did the same thing herself.

She worked long graveyard shifts at the hospital and slept away most of her days. Gwen loved her job and her work, but it left her with little free time. She had friends, but even those people weren't allowed to get very close to her. They were as numerous and casual as Facebook friends. And just as likely to be there for her when things got tough. When she'd gotten pregnant, many had scattered.

Only Adrienne really knew and understood Gwen. They both knew what it was like to hit the rock bottom of life. She had been trying to get out more lately. Adrienne was pulling her out of her shell. Cutting men out of her life had opened up some free time to do things she hadn't before. She went to more theater, toured more museums. She'd even come to the Hamptons for a relaxing, fun vacation with a group of people who were mostly strangers.

When Alex arrived and offered her another go, she hesitated, but he was a hard man to turn down when he had his sights set on you. She'd relented, given in, succumbed to the promise of a few days of pleasure without strings. And now, here she was, alone in bed because he'd had some kind of moral dilemma. Well, forget that. He had pushed her until she'd relented, and she wasn't about to be cast off like that. They were doomed to crash and burn, but that time hadn't come just yet. He owed her two more nights.

Gwen flung back the covers and marched out of her room in the tiny tank top and shorts she wore to bed. She went straight up the stairs to his bedroom and walked in without knocking or asking permission.

Alex was sitting up in bed wearing nothing but a pair of boxers and some reading glasses low on his nose. He had a pile of pillows behind him and a file open in his lap with some kind of schematic drawings. Work stuff, she assumed. He looked up in surprise when she charged in, but he didn't move. He also didn't tell her to leave. She knew he wouldn't.

She closed the door behind her and planted her hands on her hips in irritation. "What are you doing?"

Alex pulled off his glasses and tapped the paper with them. "I'm going over the final interior design drawings of my new high-rise apartment building in New Orleans."

"Is that better than making love to me?"

His hazel gaze locked on hers and he spoke without hesitation. "Not even close."

Gwen closed the gap between them, climbing onto the bed and crawling up the length of his body. Without asking permission, she stuffed the paperwork back into the folder and flopped it with a heavy thud onto the bedside table. "Then why have I been alone in my bed for the last hour?"

"Because," he said, shaking his head, "I've changed my mind about us. I pretty much twisted your arm into having this affair, but now I'm thinking it's not such a good idea. You've got that look in your eyes. I've seen it before. So I decided to take a step back before things got too serious. I mean, Adrienne is a hopeless romantic, and even she told you to stay away from me. That can't be a good sign. I don't want you to get hurt."

Gwen listened to his argument as she straddled his hips and eased back to sit astride him. The thin cotton of her pajama shorts did little to disguise the firm length of him pressing against her. She planted one hand on the oak headboard by each side of his head as though she were leaning in to kiss him, then paused a few inches away. "Since you never even bothered to ask me what I thought about all this, I'm going to say that I think that's a load of crap."

Alex's eyes widened in surprise, his whole body stiffening, but she'd left him with no escape route unless he was willing to physically fling a pregnant woman off him. His jaw tightened as he watched her, considering his words.

She didn't wait for him to answer. It wouldn't be the truth anyway, just some canned response she wasn't interested in. "I think you're the one that's afraid of getting hurt." She pressed her palm against his bare chest, covering his heart. Gwen could feel the nervous, rapid pounding in his rib cage. "So you've made up this story about protecting me so you can feel better about running before it gets too serious."

"Gwen—"

"No. I don't want to hear it. You're not just going to put me aside like all those other women. Not tonight. You owe me two more days, and I expect you to pay up."

Alex swallowed hard, his Adam's apple traveling slowly down the length of his throat and back. He watched her for several moments, not speaking. It felt like an eternity to Gwen. She held her breath. She wasn't used to being this aggressive with a man. It could blow up in her face. But at this point, she had nothing to lose.

He sat up from the pillows, bringing his face to within an inch of hers. There was a hard glint in his eyes. Gwen couldn't tell if it was anger or the rise of a challenge. His arms slinked around her, tugging her forward with a hard jerk until she was pressed against him. His breath was warm against her skin, his mouth hovering close but not yet kissing her. It sent a scorching tingle through her body, the anticipation building in her belly.

Alex was just teasing her now. Punishing her for putting him on the spot. Two could play at that game. Gwen moved her hips in a slow circle, generating a delicious friction as she ground into the firm heat that pressed insistently against her. A groan escaped his lips, and he closed his eyes when a shudder traveled through his entire body. The hands on her back fisted into tight balls at her hips. "Oh, Gwen," he whispered, his lips brushing the curve of her jaw.

"Do you still want me to go back to my room?" she asked, her pelvis continuing to swirl in agonizing circles.

She felt his fingertips reach under her tank top and lift the hem. Gwen held her arms over her head to allow him to slip the top off. He threw it to the floor, then leaned back against the pillows. His golden gaze took in every inch of her flesh from the full, bare breasts to the swell of her stomach.

With a self-satisfied grin, he said, "Unfortunately, you can't leave without your clothes."

Gwen could no longer resist the urge to kiss the smug expression from his face. Their lips met suddenly, a frantic emotional energy surging through the contact that was more powerful than anything she'd ever felt before. It was as though they were trying to devour one another. She gave in to the sensation, letting the unbridled passion overpower her.

His hands scrambled over her bare skin in a rush to touch every inch of her as though it were the first, or maybe the last, time. When their lips parted, she sucked in a much-needed breath. Alex took the opportunity to taste her breasts, the wet heat of his mouth enveloping her aching nipples and teasing them with his tongue and teeth until she cried out and writhed against him.

The grinding together of their most sensitive parts

sent a spike of need down her spine. The pulsating sensation urged her to do it again, but this time, not just to torture him. The warm pool of arousal in her belly grew with each passing second. She wanted Alex. Needed him unlike any other man, and she wasn't ashamed to admit it tonight.

"I want you, Alex," she whispered. She buried her fingers in his blond hair, tugging him closer.

"I want you, too," he said, his deep voice vibrating against the hard bone of her sternum.

"Then don't make me wait any longer."

Alex's mouth found hers again as his hands tugged at her shorts. They frantically shifted around on the bed until they were both free of the last restricting garments and he had quickly sheathed himself in the latex he relied so heavily upon.

Gwen leaned forward, then eased back, taking every inch of him inside her at an excruciatingly slow pace. With his arms still wrapped around her waist, she started rocking against him in a leisurely and easy rhythm that could go on for hours, both torturing and tempting their bodies with one wave of sensation after another.

But Alex couldn't take that for long. After a few slow, even strokes, he growled against her throat and lunged forward. Gwen was flipped onto her back, a gasp of surprise slipping from her lips. Hovering over her, he thrust into her without hesitation.

Their lovemaking was raw and intense, their bodies meeting at a fast and furious pace. Gwen let herself give in to the pleasure, indulging in the only part of Alex she would ever truly have. When their cries mingled in the air, she clung to him, part of her never wanting to let go and part of her knowing she already had.

* * *

Thoroughly exhausted, Alex fell asleep with Gwen curled against him. He woke up a few hours later, the world still dark outside his window. He was glad. He wasn't ready for the night to end quite yet. Tomorrow was the Fourth of July. He had no doubt the day would be jam-packed with grilling and sunshine, the night colored with red, white and blue explosions lighting the sky.

And then it would be over. Their last night at the house before returning to the city. No matter what he'd told Gwen, Alex didn't want any of this to be over quite yet.

Even if he broke his own rules and they carried on their relationship in Manhattan, things would be different. There would be work and responsibilities, not to mention the complications of the last few months of her pregnancy. This moment in time could never be duplicated. He wanted to savor it.

Alex let his hand glide from Gwen's bare hip down to splay his fingers across the soft skin of her belly. Feeling the baby kick the other day had been a surreal experience for him. A moment he'd never quite thought he'd have. He'd been filled with surprise and awe and respect for the woman in his arms. She was sacrificing so much for someone else.

He couldn't imagine what the next few months would be like for her. Although she put up a brave front, it was going to be harder than she'd originally anticipated. Alex saw the way she talked to the baby and lovingly stroked her stomach. Giving birth and handing that little girl away would be devastating. Part of him wanted to be the shoulder she cried on. To be there for her. It was a frightening thought. He'd never been the person that anyone depended on for emotional support. If money or humor couldn't defuse the situation, he was out of it.

But after spending the last few days with Gwen, he wanted to try. For her. The same part of him wanted to confide his secrets to her, share his dreams with her and start a life with her. The quiet voice in his head that wanted that baby to be theirs had grown louder with every day he spent here.

That same voice was screaming that it was tired of being an island. This baby wasn't theirs, but the next could be. They could have everything he had always been too afraid to hope for. If he could just let himself trust his heart over his brain for once.

Alex was so confused by the thoughts and feelings swirling around in his gut. Gwen had been right when she'd accused him of taking a step back out of fear. It seemed easier than dealing with how he felt about her. Love and everything that came with it was a scary proposition. But so was losing Gwen. He couldn't imagine not having her in his arms every night just as she was right now.

Just then, a hard thump pounded against his palm. He jumped, startled, and noticed Gwen did, too.

"Sorry," she murmured sleepily against her pillow. "Peanut is a bit of a night owl. Robert and Susan may never get another full night of sleep again once this little one shows up."

Alex stroked her belly to soothe both Gwen and the baby. He snuggled up against her and placed a kiss just behind her earlobe. The words he wanted to say lingered in his mouth for a moment before he had the nerve to speak. "What are you going to do, Gwen?"

He felt her stiffen slightly in his arms, and he tugged her closer to keep her from pulling away. If she was going to force him to face his fears, he was going to do the same. She was heading for a heartbreak that had nothing to do with him, for once.

"What do you mean?" she asked, her words still muffled against the pillow, although she was now fully awake.

"A couple months from now when you have to give her away," he clarified. "What are you going to do?"

"I'm going to watch the joy on Robert's and Susan's faces when they hold their little girl for the first time and know I did something wonderful for them. Then I'm going to check out of the hospital, catch a cab to the bar up the block from my apartment and have the tallest, coldest beer I can get my hands on."

"Gwen." The word was a question, a nudge, a warning and a touch of encouragement all rolled into one. They both knew that was not what he was asking or, even if it was, that her answer was just as scripted as his own had been earlier.

She sighed heavily, and there was a long silence before she finally answered. "What do you expect me to say? That it's going to break my heart to give Peanut away even though she's not mine to keep? That I'm going to cry alone in my hospital bed while everyone else is celebrating outside the nursery? That every time I pass a woman with a stroller I'm going to be reminded about how Robert and Susan have a beautiful life and family together and I've got nothing?"

Her words were like a knife to his gut, catching him off guard with the sharp pain. This was going to be rougher on her than he even imagined. He supposed there was nothing quite like giving away something you never had to remind you of that fact. Now he was sorry he'd asked. "Something like that."

"None of that really matters. I knew what I was signing up for with this. Sometimes the right thing to do is the hardest. I will have made a huge difference in someone else's life, and that has to be enough for me. When it's all said and done, I'll just go back to living my life the way I did before all of this happened—alone."

There was a sadness and resignation in her voice that he didn't like. They'd never discussed the possibility of being together past their stay in the Hamptons, but she sounded as though she knew he would be long gone by then. That when she handed over that baby to its parents, she would be handing away the only person in her life who loved and cared for her as much as she did for them.

It broke Alex's heart to hear her talk that way. In that moment, he wanted so badly to let himself love her. It would be so easy to do. If he was honest with himself, his heart was already halfway there. But he just couldn't commit to the last few steps. He couldn't open himself up to a fantasy that would crumble the moment he needed it the most.

"Maybe not completely alone," he offered. That was all he could do.

"Don't," she whispered, her voice heavy with tears he couldn't see. "Don't say things to make me feel better when you know it really isn't true. Lying here in the dark, I'm sure it sounds like the right thing to say. That it feels true in the moment. But you and I both know the truth when the light of day shines on it."

"I want—" he began, but stopped when Gwen rolled onto her back and held her finger to his lips.

"Just don't," she said. "Just go back to sleep before you say something we'll both regret."

* * *

Although she'd told him to sleep, Gwen couldn't do so herself. She'd spent the last few hours listening to Alex's soft, even breathing, but despite her exhaustion, her mind was spinning too quickly to sleep. Her last conversation with Alex half felt like a dream. The soft whispers and painful words felt fuzzy and surreal, but she knew she hadn't imagined them. Nor had she imagined Alex's suggestion that he might be there for her.

She hadn't let him promise. As much as she wanted it to be true, Gwen knew it never could be. She could see Alex struggling with taking the first steps to something more, but staying with her went against everything he knew. It was doomed to fail, even if his heart was in the right place. He couldn't help who he was. But she couldn't allow herself to fall for another man destined to leave.

It was one thing when that was what she wanted. Her whole life she'd sought out the wandering types. The more unobtainable, the more emotionally distant, the better.

She wasn't an expert in psychoanalysis, but she'd taken a few classes in college. It didn't take a PhD to see she had issues because of her mother and her pathetic, all-encompassing need to have a man. Gwen didn't want to be anything like her, so she picked men she knew wouldn't stay around, and it was easier when they inevitably left.

In that regard, Alex was the perfect man for her. And the worst if she truly wanted to break out of these bad habits and have a real chance at love and family.

Gwen rolled over in another failed attempt to get comfortable and tried to think about all the men she'd dated since high school. Had she ever loved any of them? No. She might've thought so or told people she did. But she held so much of herself back that it really wasn't possible to be truly, deeply in love with any of them. And if she was honest, she'd never felt half as much for any man as she did for Alex.

He took care of her because he knew how much she gave to others. He pestered her until she would smile. He knew just how to touch her and when, to get just the reaction they both wanted and needed. Alex understood Gwen in a way few people did. He'd gotten to her, scaled her protective walls and reached the heart she kept hidden.

She was in love with him. Damn it.

She expected a giddy rush of emotion at the realization, but it didn't come and she knew why. She'd gone out and done the one thing she knew she shouldn't do. What everyone, including Alex, told her not to do. It had taken her months to finally decide what she wanted in her life—a family and Alex. But those two things were mutually exclusive. She could never have Alex *and* a family. But for some reason she'd let him in, and what was done, was done.

Gwen loved Alex.

And he, despite his protests, felt something for her. She knew it. She could feel it in his hesitation. If he didn't care about her, he wouldn't have walked away tonight. But in her heart, she knew that regardless of how he felt, their relationship was doomed. How could she be the one to tame Alex when so many others had failed?

She wouldn't. She'd just get hurt. Dating guys who didn't stick around was one thing. Loving the guy was another matter. She'd taken a break from her merry-go-round of self-destructive relationships only to find herself in deeper than she'd ever been before.

When the first glow of daylight began to creep into his room, she sat up in bed. Alex was still soundly sleeping beside her. She realized, looking at him, that she'd never really seen him asleep before. He always woke up before she did.

A lock of dark golden hair lay across one of his eyes. The cocky, suave persona was put away while he slept. His face was relaxed, peaceful…vulnerable. That was certainly a new expression for him. While he occasionally appeared concerned or serious, she'd never once seen his guard down like this. There were flashes of it when he'd looked at her that first night and realized he'd forgotten the condom. But it had vanished in an instant.

Part of her wanted to reach out and stroke the line of his jaw and the curves of his lips, but that would wake him up and ruin it. Instead, she lay there for a few more minutes, committing that face to memory before she got up.

Finally, she slipped out of bed and collected her clothes, pulling them on and heading to her own room. Gwen paused in the doorway as she left, looking back one last time at Alex asleep in his bed. She'd meant only to go downstairs, but a part of her knew she was walking away from more than just Alex's bedroom.

With a sigh, she whispered, "Goodbye, Alex," and pulled the door shut behind her.

Ten

Gwen had nearly reached the bottom of the stairs when a bit of movement caught her eye.

Startled, she turned and found Sabine in the living room. She was wearing tight yellow workout clothes and poised on one foot on a squishy blue mat. Her arms were over her head, and the other knee was bent out to the side, the sole of her foot pressing into her thigh. She looked like some kind of neon-yellow flamingo.

"Good morning," Sabine said without stumbling from her one-legged pose.

"I'm sorry to interrupt," Gwen said sheepishly. She hadn't expected to see anyone on her way back to her room. Especially not at this hour of morning.

"You're not." Sabine smiled and brought her foot back to the floor. "I've been lazy about my yoga while I've been here, and I'm paying for it. I decided to get up before everyone to stretch. My next class back I'll be stiff as a board, and all my students will laugh at me."

Gwen paused at the bottom of the staircase. "You teach yoga? I thought you worked in Adrienne's boutique."

Sabine nodded and knelt down onto her mat. "The yoga is a part-time thing. I teach a couple evening classes and a prenatal one on Saturday mornings." She gestured toward Gwen. "You should come. When I was pregnant, my doctor recommended a prenatal yoga class, and after it, I felt good for the first time in months. After I had my son, I stuck with it, and it really helped me get back into shape."

"I'd love to give that a try. Not only to get in shape, but to help me fill some of the hours. After." When she was alone again.

Sabine nodded sympathetically. "You're doing a wonderful thing, you know? I shouldn't have said what I did the other day about how I could never do something like that. It was thoughtless of me, considering how hard it must be for you and you're doing it anyway."

Gwen shook her head dismissively. "Don't worry about it. It is more difficult than I expected and certainly not something just anyone could do. But it will be worth it."

"Right." Sabine smiled and her purple-striped ponytail swung behind her. "Would you like to try some stretches now?"

Sabine reached into her duffel bag and pulled out a second mat, this one a bright pink. She rolled it out beside her and patted it in invitation. "Just a couple for you to do at home until you can get to a class."

Gwen climbed onto the mat and worked through a set of poses with Sabine that not only made the pain in her back disappear, but stretched out all her other stiff muscles and brought a touch of sweat to her brow. When they were done, she sat back on her heels to do some deep breathing. Going through the motions had cleared her head remarkably. She never imagined something like that could help her think, but if stress and pain were clouding her thoughts, it made perfect sense.

"Can I ask you a personal question?"

"Sure," Sabine said. "I don't have many secrets."

Gwen was a bit ashamed to ask, but she needed someone to talk to about Alex, someone with some distance. She got the feeling that Sabine had some experience where doomed relationships were concerned. "What happened with your son's father?"

"We were just wrong for each other. Attraction trumped all that at first, but it didn't take long to realize it wasn't going to work between us. He was rich, I was poor. He was preoccupied with running his business. I just wanted to enjoy life. It almost killed me, but I broke it off after only a few weeks. I knew it would only get worse the longer I waited. It wasn't until much later that I realized I was already pregnant with his child."

"He didn't want the baby?"

Sabine frowned. "Oh, I'm sure he'd want the baby. That's why I never told him." She shook her head sadly. "I know it sounds like a horrible thing to do. But when I said he was a rich businessman, I also meant powerful, arrogant and controlling. I didn't want Jared to be a pawn in his empire. I refused to give Gavin the opportunity to sue me for full custody just so my son could be raised by nannies and go to boarding school. Honestly, I'm surprised I've gone this long without him showing up at my doorstep demanding his son."

Gwen couldn't help but shake her head in wonder. It

seemed like everyone had their own messes in life to clean up. "That must be stressful, knowing at any time that he could find out."

"You have no idea. But I know leaving was the right choice, so I try to focus on living my life. I'm raising Jared the best I can and making sure he feels loved and wanted. He shouldn't have to suffer because I'm a failure at relationships."

Sabine climbed to her feet and held out a hand to help Gwen up. "Love can be wonderful, but it can also be destructive. I loved Gavin. It was a fierce, passionate romance, but I loved myself too much to lose who I was to him. I couldn't sit around and wait for him to crush my spirit."

"You did the right thing," Gwen said.

"Yes. It's important not to settle," Sabine agreed. "Remember that."

Gwen nodded. It was solid advice, but it sent her mind spinning with what it meant for her after her latest revelation about loving Alex. "Thank you for the advice. And the yoga."

Sabine smiled and waved it off as Gwen disappeared toward her room. Although she eyed the bed when she shut the door, the yoga had invigorated her, and she opted for a hot shower instead.

Gwen felt ashamed for misjudging Sabine that first day. She should know better than to label someone because of their appearance. Perhaps she'd make a point to call her for lunch one day after Peanut was born. It could be one of her steps toward making some real friends and having a life outside work. And she would definitely look into that yoga class. Those poses had worked wonders on her body.

Maybe in time it would also help her with peace of

mind. A little meditation and removal of brain clutter couldn't hurt, at least. The hot water of the shower helped her body relax, but her mind was still spinning a hundred miles an hour from their conversation. She wished she could hook a vacuum to her ear and suck out all the negative thoughts.

Unfortunately, she just wasn't a "glass half-full" kind of girl. Gwen liked to think of herself as a "hope for the best, but plan for the worst" type. What did that mean for her relationship with Alex? That she hoped they'd have a good time together and her heart wouldn't be crushed when he inevitably left?

With a sigh, she rinsed her hair a final time and closed her eyes. That was ridiculous. How could a relationship be solid when she had such a large escape hatch?

It couldn't. And that was part of the problem.

Sabine was right. Gwen shouldn't settle. If she wanted a marriage and family with a great man, she could have it. If it couldn't be with Alex, she needed to accept that. But she shouldn't just sit around and wait for the day Alex left. Each minute she spent with him would make the ending that much more painful, not to mention putting off her chance to meet the right kind of guy. She needed to be proactive. To take control of her life. Right now.

Gwen was putting the last of her things in her suitcase when there was a soft tap at the door. She prayed it wasn't Alex. She wasn't quite sure what she'd say if he saw her packing to leave. It wasn't that long ago that he'd called her a chicken, and he was right. She didn't know how to deal with this.

"It's Adrienne," a voice called through the door.

"Come in." Gwen tossed her toiletry bag into the case and closed it as the door opened.

Adrienne slipped in and shut the door behind her. "You're leaving." It wasn't a question. She knew Gwen well enough to know exactly what was going on without having to ask. The story would be fully hashed out over dinner in a few weeks, when the pain wasn't so fresh and she had enough distance to talk about it.

"I have to. I'm sorry if this ruins your plans for today."

"It wouldn't matter if it did. Do you need me or Will to drive you back?"

"All the way to Manhattan? No, don't be silly. I don't want either of you to cut your vacation short on my account. But I could use a ride to the train station or maybe a jitney stop. Whatever is closer."

"Absolutely. The Hampton Jitney stops down on Main Street. You can probably book a ticket on your phone. I'll just go get my keys."

Gwen zipped her bag and turned to her best friend. Unwelcome tears had gathered in her eyes, but she refused to shed them. She wasn't about to cry while *she* left *him*. That wasn't how it worked. "Thank you."

Adrienne rushed forward and swept Gwen into a hug. "Oh, Gwen," she lamented. "I'm so sorry. I've worried about you ever since I found out what happened."

"I'm so stupid. I can't believe I let myself… I never should've…"

"Fallen in love?"

Gwen pulled away and sniffed back the tears. "With Alexander Stanton! I seriously need therapy or somethin'. I know that if I ever want a real, healthy relationship, I've gotta stop doing this to myself. So I'm leaving. I'm starting fresh. I'm going to have this baby and start living a life open to the possibilities of real love. I deserve happiness."

"Without question. And I have no doubt you'll find it. I'll meet you out front in a minute." Adrienne went out to the kitchen and left Gwen alone for a moment.

She reached over to the dresser and the silver charm bracelet still lying there. She went to slip it on, then paused. She didn't need Alex's gift to protect her anymore. She was open to love and possibilities. Just not with him. Gwen scooped the bracelet up and grabbed her suitcase off the bed.

When she met Adrienne in the living room, she had her purse and keys in hand. "Do you want to leave him a note or something?"

Gwen shook her head. "I doubt he's ever left a note for any of the women he's left. I don't know what I'd put on there anyway." Gwen held out the bracelet to Adrienne. "Could you just give him this and tell him I had to go? He's a smart enough guy to figure out the rest."

Adrienne nodded and held open the front door. They loaded the Land Rover and pulled out of the driveway.

"I've got my ticket booked for eight this morning," Gwen said as they stopped in front of the local movie theater. It was closed at this hour of the morning, and there was almost no one around.

Adrienne glanced down at her watch. "You shouldn't have too long to wait then. Do you want me to stay here with you until it comes?"

"No, I'm fine. You go back to the house and continue having a good vacation with your friends. I expect you to have some more excellent fireworks tonight."

Adrienne nodded and leaned in to give her friend another hug. "Be safe. And call me when you get back to your apartment so I won't worry."

"I will."

Gwen slipped out the car door and pulled her bag from the backseat. The morning sun had just begun shining in earnest as she rolled her suitcase over to the park bench to wait for the bus. She gave a quick wave to Adrienne as she pulled away. Once the car disappeared out of sight, she felt a weight lifted from her chest.

It was just as well she hadn't driven herself. This way, she couldn't lose her nerve and circle back to him.

Alex stood in Gwen's empty bedroom, his eyes burrowing into the cold, empty bed where he'd expected to find her sleeping. The drawers were empty, the toothbrush missing from the counter by the sink. He wasn't quite sure how to process all of this.

He'd woken up alone and thought nothing of it. Alex had slipped out of Gwen's room each night to return to his own before everyone got up. He figured she'd done the same. He'd showered, dressed and headed downstairs in anticipation of the typical Fourth of July activities. He had no reason to think anything was wrong.

Everyone but Gwen was out by the pool, so he'd gone to her room to see if she'd overslept. It was obvious now that she hadn't. She'd woken up early and gotten a head start on them all.

His mind raced through last night and everything that had happened. Gwen had seemed determined not to let Alex pull away from her. And yet today, she was gone. She'd left him without saying a word. What had happened from the time she charged into his room to the moment she'd crept out that would make her decide to go so suddenly?

A dull ache settled in his chest when he sucked

in a breath and the air still smelled like her lavender shampoo.

She'd left him.

Something about the whole thing didn't sit right with him. Maybe it was because Alex had never been left by a woman before. He was always the first to go, the first to decide that things weren't working out. He'd broken it off with his first girlfriend, Tiffany Atwell, in seventh grade after the spring formal, and it was a trend that had continued until now.

Just one more thing that set Gwen apart. For the first time, he'd been left wanting more.

He took a few steps into the room, smoothing his hand over the comforter. It was cold. She'd been gone a while. Confused, Alex sat down on the edge of the bed and stared into the bathroom where her swimsuit should be hanging.

The memory of her in that tiny navy bikini hit him in the gut like a truck. It felt as if the wind had been knocked out of him, his breath stuck in his throat. His chest tightened, the dull ache sharpening to an acute pain.

So this is what it felt like to be dumped, he thought. It sucked. No wonder he'd received so many nasty voice mails and texts over the years from his exes.

A glance at the bedside stand revealed a stray peppermint left behind the base of the lamp. He reached out for it, unwrapping the candy and putting it in his mouth. The strong, fresh bite instantly brought to mind memories of her kisses. Their first on the dance floor at the reception. The one on the pier. In the pool. His mind was suddenly driven to remember them all and savor them as his last.

Not once in his life had he ever ended a relationship

and worried later about forgetting a woman's kisses. But remembering Gwen's seemed important. Too important.

"She left early this morning."

Alex's head snapped to the doorway, where Adrienne was standing, watching him. Her arms were crossed over her chest, but she didn't seem angry. Somehow he expected that Adrienne would lay the blame at his feet for hurting Gwen and driving her away. But there was only sadness in her green eyes.

"Why? I don't understand."

"I think Gwen decided it was for the best. She knew that you two didn't have a future together, and prolonging it was just too painful for her. She's got a bad habit of falling in love with the wrong kind of guy."

"Love?" Alex perked up at Adrienne's choice of words. He hadn't expected to hear that at all. "She's in love with me?"

Her eyes widened as she stumbled for a moment to take back what she'd said. "I…that, I mean…that was just a generalization. I don't know if she loves you or not."

Will was right. He'd said once that Adrienne was a terrible liar. The truth was painted across her face. She'd let her best friend's secret slip. Alex had slowly regained the ability to breathe over the last few minutes, but suddenly the air caught in his lungs, and his heart stilled in his chest. Gwen was in love with him. In love. With him.

And yet, she was gone just the same.

Alex had heard a few women tell him that in his lifetime. Usually as part of a plea to make him reconsider staying. It never worked, because he knew their words were as authentic as their hair color.

But he wanted to hear Gwen say the words to him. And he'd lost his chance.

"Why would she leave if she loved me?"

Adrienne walked into the room and sat down on the bed beside Alex. "She finally decided she wants a real, loving relationship and to start her own family. You and I both know that you're not willing to give her the life she wants. And she knows it, too. So as much as it hurt, she knew she needed to leave before it just got worse."

Alex understood. But usually he was the one to see it in the woman, and he would be the one to leave.

"She asked me to give you this." Adrienne reached out and placed Gwen's silver charm bracelet in his hand.

He closed his fist around the cold metal. The one thing Alex understood about being with Gwen was that he never knew where he stood with her. She was unlike any woman he'd ever met, and her mere existence challenged him every day. It made sense that she would be the first to leave him feeling like crap when it was over.

"Are you going to be okay, Alex?" Adrienne looked at him with concern in her eyes that he wasn't used to seeing. At least, not directed at him.

"Me? Oh yeah," he assured her, although the words sounded hollow to his ears. "You know me."

She nodded and patted his knee, but he could tell there was a part of her that was just humoring him. "I'm making buttermilk waffles with strawberries for brunch, so don't stay in here too long or Will and Jack will eat them all."

Alex pasted on one of his smiles. "I'll be out in just a minute."

Adrienne slipped from the room, pulling the door closed to give him some privacy with his thoughts. It didn't take much time for him to realize he didn't want to be alone in Gwen's room any longer. He got up quickly, heading up the stairs to return to his own private sanctuary.

Alone in his room, he felt a bit of the tightness in his chest ease up. The air in here didn't smell like her, which helped. At least until he spied the bundle of dried-up roses sitting on his dresser. When Gwen had returned them, he hadn't known what to do with the flowers, so he'd let them sit. Just as he didn't know what to do with the bracelet she no longer wanted.

Without hesitation, Alex swung his arm across the dresser top, forcefully clearing it and flinging the flowers, the charm bracelet and anything else sitting up there scattering across the floor. Now he wouldn't have to look at it and think of her.

He expected to feel better when everything crashed to the ground, but he didn't. Fortunately, he had an idea of what would help.

If Alex knew anything, it was how to bounce back after a breakup. Playing for the "dumped" team didn't change what happened next.

He'd enjoy the rest of his holiday with his friends. Drink some beers, shoot some fireworks. He would drive back to the city with the top down and soak in the warm summer sunshine. In Manhattan, he'd get a new haircut, buy a new suit and spend a few nights on the town in his favorite haunts. Maybe he'd meet a nice lady to distract him from thinking of Gwen. Perhaps he'd meet a couple ladies. Whatever it took.

Either way, life would get back to normal once he returned to the city. He could focus on work, racquetball, everything, anything, but Gwen. And before too long, she would be a distant memory, just like the others.

Eleven

"Nurse Wright?"

Gwen snapped out of her fog to see one of the doctors on rotation looking at her curiously. "I'm sorry. What did you need?"

Dr. Ellis grinned. "Still in a vacation haze, eh, Gwen?"

She forced a smile and shrugged. "Something like that."

He proceeded to rattle off a list of things she needed to do for one of the patients he'd just checked on. She pulled the woman's file and made a note of it on her chart. "Consider it done."

Pleased, he turned and headed down the hallway. Gwen watched him walk away, thinking about how Dr. Ellis had a smile that reminded her of Alex. The simple thought brought tentative tears to her eyes that she refused to shed.

By the time he'd disappeared around the corner, there was nothing left in her memory but Alex's crooked, sly grin. Unfortunately, that wouldn't help her treat Mrs. Maghee. She glanced down at her notes, relieved. She didn't remember a thing Dr. Ellis had told her, but she'd copied down every word.

Gwen sat back in her rolling office chair behind the nurses' station, disgusted. She needed to get it together. She left him. She needed to stop moping and focus. Her job was important. Her patients depended on her. She couldn't wander around in a lovesick daze.

It had been nearly two weeks since she'd returned home from the Hamptons. Life had gone back to normal. At least, as close as it could be to how life was before she'd gone on vacation. But even in her old routines, something was different.

She was different.

Gwen had always told herself that she lived and breathed her job because she loved it so much. That she didn't need love and family, because her work was so important and fulfilling. Her patients were her family. Her relationship was with the hospital.

As she looked around the sterile halls with the mint-green-and-white tile floors, it was clear the honeymoon of this marriage was over. It wasn't enough for her anymore. She wasn't about to abandon her work, but her universe wasn't going to revolve around it any longer.

When she'd made the decision to leave early and put her relationship with Alex behind her, she'd made a choice to start her life anew. At first, she'd thought packing her bags and walking out would be the hardest part. Once she'd arrived back in Manhattan, she'd realized that was just the first of many difficult steps ahead of her. She had a lifetime of bad habits to break if she wanted to be happy.

But she would do it. The one thing Gwen was determined to do was carry on. She might be the emotional equivalent of a tin man right now, but that wasn't going to stop her. Sabine was right. Gwen deserved a man who would love her and give her all the things she wanted in life, without having to settle.

The last few months carrying Peanut and the few days in the Hamptons with Alex had made it clear that what she wanted was a family of her own. She couldn't keep Alex, and she couldn't keep this baby, but she could have that and more with someone who cared enough to stick around.

Being open to love didn't make her like her mother. And every guy out there was not like her father. Or Alex. There were good men out there who would stay. Like Will. And Robert. She needed to put her issues in a box at the top of the closet and find the right kind of man for her.

A twinge of pain seized Gwen's back. She winced and tried to soothe it with her hand, but it didn't do much good. It was doubtful that even yoga would help. It really had been bothering her the last few hours. Every ten minutes or so, it would flare up something fierce. She must've slept wrong last night. She hadn't slept very well since she'd gotten home. Suddenly the sounds of the city kept her awake, when they'd never bothered her before. Or maybe it was the vacant spot in the bed beside her.

Gwen sighed and moved her hand to her belly. The back pain was a reminder that she had some time to kill—about four months—before she would be ready to put herself back on the market. She hadn't officially resumed her man-break, but if her time in the Hamptons had taught her nothing else, it was that pregnancy made relationships infinitely more complicated. It brought up all these confusing feelings that didn't help an already tricky situation.

But she was determined. She was going to see this surrogacy through and start her new life as the new Gwen. Open, terrified, but unwavering Gwen. She could do this.

"Mama Gwen, are you feeling okay? You look a little pale." The head nurse, a large and nurturing grandmother type named Wilma, approached the nurses' station, a frown lining her plump face.

Once again, Gwen pasted on a smile to cover up the pain. She wasn't about to worry Wilma with her sad tales of heartache and back pain. "I'm fine. Just a little tired. I think I got used to regular hours while I was on vacation."

"Daylight is overrated. Are you sure you're all right?"

Gwen started to nod but was interrupted by a sharp pain that radiated across her abdomen. This one put the backache to shame. She couldn't help the gasp as she clutched her stomach and looked up at Wilma with wide, confused eyes. "Maybe not. Wow, that hurts."

Wilma frowned, coming around the counter faster than one would've expected of a woman of her age and size. She knelt down in front of Gwen to examine her more closely. "Have you had a backache?"

Gwen nodded, biting her lip to keep from yelping and waking up her patients.

"Any spotting?"

"A little at my last lunch break. But that's normal, isn't it?"

"It can be. But not when you add it all together. How many weeks are you now?"

"Almost twenty-five."

Wilma frowned again. "That's about twelve weeks fewer than I'd like. I haven't worked in L and D for about twenty years, but this kind of stuff doesn't change. Mama, I hate to say this, but I think you're going into premature labor."

Alex strode into the temporary office space he leased as the headquarters for his latest building project. It was about a block away from the actual build site of the apartment high-rise, so it was both convenient and spacious for their needs. A local office supply had rented them the furniture, and a temp agency provided a receptionist for the front desk and janitorial staff.

Their temporary admin, Lisa, looked up as he came through the doors, placing a call on hold. "Good morning, Mr. Stanton. I wasn't expecting to see you this morning. Does Miss Jacobs know you're here?"

Alex chuckled softly to himself. "No, I don't believe Tabitha is expecting me." Actually, he knew she wasn't. He'd deliberately not told his project manager he was coming to New Orleans. She was competent, driven, successful... All the things he wanted in an employee. Normally, this meant he could get engaged with the fun, creative parts of starting a new real estate project, then leave her to actually execute the details. That was how he liked it.

Of course, normally, he wasn't hell-bent on getting out of Manhattan before he did something stupid he would regret. He already had enough regrets as it was; he didn't need any more. Especially where Gwen was concerned.

In the weeks since he'd left the Hamptons, he'd tried to continue on with his life as usual, but everything felt wrong somehow. The women were disinteresting, the jokes flat, the drinks bitter or tasteless. Will even beat him at racquetball for the first time. He found himself wandering through his empty penthouse without purpose. As much as he didn't want to admit it, his life didn't seem to work without Gwen in it anymore.

He kept finding himself dialing her number but unable to hit the call button. Instead he would just hang up. Gwen had left him out of self-preservation. Calling her was the worst thing he could do. Especially if he wasn't willing to offer her what she wanted.

And yet, he'd find the phone in his hand again, or ask his driver to cruise past her apartment or the hospital in the hope he'd catch a glimpse of her walking outside.

No luck, so far.

But he was playing with fire. The last time he'd needed to get Gwen out of his head, he'd flown to New Orleans and started this project. It seemed like the best course of action now as well. So he'd gotten on a plane and headed down here unannounced.

"Shall I call and let her know you're here?"

"That won't be necessary, Lisa. I'd like to surprise her."

The look on Lisa's face made it painfully obvious that she knew Tabitha very well. Surprises were not on the top of the list of things she enjoyed. Even a good surprise could piss her off because it messed with her schedule.

That just made it all the more fun.

Although he normally was not involved much past the planning stage, he still maintained an office of his own at each site. He buzzed past Lisa and headed straight for his long-abandoned desk. Flipping on the light, he set down his laptop bag, threw his coat over his chair and headed to the kitchen. He poured a cup of coffee into one of the paper cups and snatched an apple fritter from a pink bakery box on the counter.

Alex took the fritter and carried it down the hall with his coffee. Without ceremony, he walked into Tabitha's office and sat down in her guest chair to eat his breakfast.

She was busily typing at her computer, her pale red-gold hair pulled into a tight bun and her curves stuffed into one of her favorite, unflattering business suits. He could tell by her pinched expression that she knew someone was there, but she hadn't torn her eyes from the screen to see who.

The moment she did look, her expression was a jolt of pure joy he was in sore need of. He'd felt like hell since he'd left the Hamptons. Harassing his project manager was one of his small pleasures in life.

"Alex? I mean, Mr. Stanton? What are you doing here? Is there a problem?"

"Yes," he said, trying to maintain a straight face. "I am very concerned to report a severe shortage of cream-filled doughnuts in this office. It's shameful."

Tabitha's wide violet-blue eyes narrowed at him as her initial panic faded to irritation. "What are you doing here, Alex? In the last six years and seven projects I've executed for you, not once have you shown up during the build phase."

"Can't I come check on how things are going?"

Tabitha sighed and pushed an imaginary loose strand of hair behind her ear. "Of course. And everything is fine. Great. We're ahead of schedule. Under budget. We've secured contracts for over half the units already, and we're on track to being completely sold out before the last inch of drywall is painted."

Alex nodded, pleased with the progress. "You're worth every penny I pay you, Tabitha."

"I'm probably worth a few more than you pay me."

He had to admit he liked her sass. He'd date her if it wouldn't ruin their perfect work situation. Even a man with a reputation like his had boundaries. No ex-anythings of friends, no sisters of friends, no employees and no nurses. That last one was a new addition.

"Remind me to give you a raise when this project is done, then."

Tabitha opened up her calendar software, typed a note into her computer and nodded. "Done. Now, tell me why you're really here. Who is she? Is it the same woman you were down here hiding from last time?"

"I was not hiding," Alex said, setting his coffee cup forcefully on the edge of her desk.

Tabitha shrugged off his display of male aggression, picking her smartphone up off the desk as it started to buzz. Her eyes never left the small screen as she spoke to her boss. "Call it what you like. You were completely unfocused when you were here before. I assumed it was a woman."

Defeated, Alex took a bite of his fritter. "It was."

"And this time?"

"Same one."

This finally caught Tabitha's attention. Her eyebrow arched curiously at him. "Sounds serious."

"It's not. I don't *do* serious."

"Which explains why you're here with me instead of there with her."

Damn his ability to hire smart, capable women. They saw far more than he wanted them to see. "Possibly."

Tabitha sighed and pushed up from her chair. "I've got an on-site meeting with the head contractor in ten minutes. Are you going to walk down there with me?"

Alex drank the last of his coffee and tossed his napkin into her trash can. "Yes," he said with the last mouthful of apple fritter garbling his words.

She nodded and marched out the door. He followed behind Tabitha, finding her waiting impatiently at the elevator. "So how long are you going to be around?" she asked as they waited for the car to arrive at their floor.

Honestly, Alex wasn't really sure. How long did it take to get over a woman? He'd never been involved enough with one to know. But he rounded up to goad his project manager. "A couple weeks at least."

Tabitha didn't even have the decency to muffle the groan of displeasure as the elevator doors opened.

There were no more discussions once they reached the street. The central business district was busy and loud this time of day, reminding Alex of Manhattan. Part of their building design centered around heavily insulated walls and double-paned windows specifically crafted for soundproofing. You could close your eyes and convince yourself you were in the country, it was so quiet. No sirens, no honking, no neighbors' music or arguing.

The people buying his apartments wanted to be at the center of the New Orleans excitement and energy but wanted to keep the luxury and security they were accustomed to. Stanton Towers would provide all of that for an astronomical fee, and yet, he usually had waiting lists of well-off clients chomping at the bit to get into one of his facilities.

The site was currently a mess of construction. Alex was typically not involved in this phase. Cement and jackhammers were not of interest to him. Right now, the steel skeleton of the high-rise stretched nearly ten stories in the air. That was about two-thirds of its final height. A large chain-link fence enclosed the site and protected passersby from the heavy equipment and chaos surrounding the project.

Tabitha paused outside the fence and grabbed a hard hat. She handed one over to Alex, then glanced down at his shoes. "I hope those aren't expensive."

"Of course they are," he responded irritably, then realized they were about to walk through the dirt and mud to the large trailer where the site manager operated. He glanced down at Tabitha's shoes, expecting heels, and found that with her suit, she was wearing steel-toed work boots. You didn't see that every day, but she was nothing if not prepared.

"Nice look. Do you wear those shoes on the first date?" he asked as they started off to the trailer.

Tabitha frowned. "I keep these at the office for trips like this. My other shoes are tucked safely under my desk for when I get back. And for any dates that might pop up. If you ever stuck around for the dirty work, you'd have seen these already."

Alex tried to step carefully the first few feet, then realized Tabitha would leave him in her dust before too long. She was a no-nonsense woman. Probably just the kind to give him the straight answers he needed right now. The question was whether or not he wanted to hear it. "Tabitha, you're a woman," he said.

"Last time I checked," she said, drily.

"Let me ask you something about women."

"Oh, lord," she groaned, turning in her boots to face him. "I don't have time for this, Alex, so here's a quick tip. Whatever you've done, apologize and beg her to take you back."

"What makes you think I did something?"

Tabitha didn't respond, but crossed her arms over her chest and sighed heavily.

"Okay, I know I'm typically guilty of something, but this time *she* left *me*."

Alex regretted having this conversation with Tabitha immediately. Watching his uptight, driven manager crumble into a fit of hysterical laughter was too much. "You... got...*dumped?*" she asked between hard-fought breaths.

"Will you stop laughing? This is serious. She's in love with me," he blurted out.

The laughter faded and Tabitha fought to hold her composure. "Poor woman. Running was probably the right choice. But don't act like you didn't give her a reason to leave."

"She decided I was a flight risk if I found out the truth, and she left before I could."

"You *are* a flight risk. And a jerk if you're even considering chasing after her if you're not serious about this. Do you love her, Alex?"

That was the sixty-five-thousand-dollar question. He thought he didn't believe in love. That if it existed, he was immune to it. But these last few weeks without Gwen had been absolute torture. He'd lain awake at night, thinking about the time they'd spent together in that very bed. Every show on television or song on the radio somehow reminded him of her. And the worst part was this constant, dull ache in his chest that refused to go away no matter how many antacids he took.

Was that what love felt like? He had no clue. No basis for comparison. All he knew was that he'd never felt like this after a relationship ended. If this was love, it was no wonder Gwen opted to leave when she had realized she loved him. Love could seriously suck when things weren't going right. He could only hope it felt better when the relationship was doing well.

"I don't know. I've never been in love before. But I can't stop thinking about her. I'm absolutely miserable."

"I hate to tell you this, but it sounds like love to me."

Alex's heart skipped a beat in his chest when Tabitha confirmed the thought that had been plaguing him for days. Love. *Love* was a big, scary word for a guy like Alex. Just saying it out loud might break him out in hives. He wasn't programmed for monogamy. He didn't even know what step to take next. "But I don't know how to fix things between us. No matter what I say, Gwen will never trust me to stay."

Tabitha glanced down at her watch, then back at Alex. "Here's your last tip, then I'm going into that trailer for my meeting, alone. This woman loves you. I have no idea why. If you love her, you need to go to her and beg her to give her a chance to prove her wrong. Offer her everything she wants and *deliver* on it."

Alex swallowed hard. Going to Gwen would mean offering everything he'd avoided his whole life: commitment, love, trust. And those things he'd never thought he wanted: marriage, children, domesticity. But he wanted it with her. If she'd give him the opportunity to try.

"You're right."

"Of course I'm right. Now, get your ass on a plane back to New York and get out of my hair. I don't want to see you again until the final walk-through before the ribbon-cutting ceremony."

Tabitha turned on her heel and disappeared, leaving

Alex to make his way back through the obstacle course of the construction site.

He took a different route, this time heading back toward his hotel instead of the office. He needed some time to process what Tabitha had said. In a matter of minutes, her take-no-prisoners attitude had cut through all the mental crap he'd been bogged down in for days. He loved Gwen. He knew that now. And if he wanted her, he had to be willing to offer her the life and the family she deserved.

But he had to do something to prove to her that he was serious. He needed to knock on her door with an engagement ring in his hands. But not just any ring. Gwen wouldn't be convinced by some vulgar and generic display of diamonds. She'd want something authentic. Something that was distinctly hers. Gwen was like no other woman, and she deserved a ring like no other. Knowing he'd put the thought into the purchase would be what made the difference for her.

Alex started on the hunt for a jewelry store. With the help of his phone, he located and rejected several shops. They all had fine products, but nothing in the store said Gwen. Looking down on his phone, he noticed there was an antiques and estate jeweler a couple blocks past the hotel. Maybe that was what he needed. A vintage piece.

By the time he reached the shop window, he'd been wandering around New Orleans for more than two hours. Waiting to catch his breath before he went inside, he admired the front display. A large and varied collection of jewelry was in the window, protected by decorative but sturdy wrought-iron bars.

After hours of fruitless searches, he was surprised to find that one of the rings called to him immediately. He leaned in to look closer. The platinum-and-gold antique filigree setting was inset with tiny diamonds around the thin band. In the center was a large yellow oval-cut stone in a ring of additional tiny diamonds.

It was bright and sunny yet extremely detailed and complicated. It was Gwen in jewel form. Curious, he went inside the store and summoned the old man behind the counter. He unlocked the case and took the ring with him back to the white pad where he displayed jewelry for buyers.

"You have a good eye. It's the best piece in my whole shop. I suppose most people don't realize what it is or think it's citrine or some type of costume jewelry."

Alex frowned. "What is it?"

"A three-carat canary diamond. I bought it thirty-five years ago from the estate auction of an old New Orleans family. Their great-great-grandfather brought it here from France in the 1760s. Rumor is it was given as a gift to a lover of King Louis the Sixteenth, who popularized the use of platinum in Europe. I've got bulletproof glass and bars on the windows for a reason, sonny."

It was beautiful, rare and priceless. Alex couldn't be sure how much of the old man's yarn was truth and how much was fiction to justify the price, but it didn't really matter as long as the certification paperwork held up. If he was lucky, Gwen might not even know how valuable a ring she was wearing. If she accepted it. And he had no guarantee that she would. "I'll take it."

The old man's eyes widened. "Don't you want to know how much it is?"

Alex shrugged. "It doesn't matter."

"Well," he chuckled, "okay then. I'll box this up and get the paperwork for it together. You feel free to look around while you wait, and see if there's anything else you might need at an irrelevant price."

A few minutes later, Alex walked out of the store with the ring securely tucked into the breast pocket of his suit coat. He moved with more purpose now. He finally had some direction. He was going back to New York. He was going to tell Gwen that he loved her. That he wanted to marry her. Have children with her. That he wouldn't get scared and run away, and he wasn't going to let her run, either.

He could only hope that, after everything that had happened, she would believe him.

Twelve

Alex made a quick stop at his hotel. He grabbed his things, checked out and headed straight to the office. He asked Lisa to get on the phone and change his flight, and he grabbed his laptop from his desk. Thirty minutes later, he was downstairs waiting for the car to take him to the airport.

When his phone rang, he almost ignored it. He was too hyped up on love and adrenaline to let business or family drama bring him down. But he couldn't help looking to see who it was. It was Adrienne's cell phone.

Alex frowned and knew he had to answer. Adrienne never called him. Only Will. "Adrienne," he said, tentatively.

"Where are you, Alex?"

"I'm in New Orleans. But I'm getting on a flight back to LaGuardia shortly."

"Why? Did someone already call you?"

"Call me? No. About what?"

"About Gwen."

Alex's heart sank like a stone in his chest. Why would someone call him about Gwen? "What about her? Is she okay? Has something happened? Is the baby okay?"

Adrienne was silent on the phone for half a heartbeat, making Alex almost ready to leap through the receiver and shake her until she told him what was going on. "They're both fine...now."

He breathed a ragged sigh of relief, but he could tell there was more to the story. "What's happened?"

"She went into premature labor while she was at work last night. Luckily, her supervisor realized what was happening and took her downstairs. They immediately admitted her."

"Labor? What? She's only, like, six months along. Why would she have gone into labor?"

"I know. They're not sure why it happened, because she has so many weeks left and no real risk factors. That's why it's so serious. They've got her on some very strong intravenous medication to stop the contractions. They seem to have done the trick for now. But the next few months will be rough. She's going to be on mandatory bed rest. She has to take leave from work, and she won't be able to afford to keep her apartment on her reduced pay. Anything could start up the contractions again, and if her water breaks, they'll have to risk delivery no matter how far along she is."

Alex gripped his skull with his free hand. Picturing Gwen alone in a hospital bed, fearful for the baby's life, was eating him up inside. He felt helpless. "What can I do?"

"Come back. She'll kill me for doing this, but if you care at all for her, come back to New York. Be here for her. She'd never admit it, but she needs you to get through this. I lied the day she left the Hamptons, because I was trying to protect her. Gwen loves you, Alex. She's just scared of being hurt."

"I know," he said solemnly. "I love her, too."

Adrienne muttered a soft curse. "You love her? Really? The mighty Alexander Stanton has fallen?"

Alex supposed he deserved all this, but he would be the willing butt of all the jokes after he was back and he knew Gwen and the baby were safe. "Yes. I'm in love with her. That's why I was coming back to New York. I wanted to tell her that I wasn't going to let her run away from us. My flight gets in this afternoon. I'll go straight to the hospital from there."

"Call me when you get here, and I'll get you her new room number. They're moving her to a regular room this afternoon."

Alex said goodbye and hung up the phone. He couldn't get to New York fast enough. Gwen was in the hospital. Both her life and the baby's were potentially in danger. She was stable now, but what if something horrible happened and he never got to tell her how he felt? What if she lost the baby and he was a thousand miles away hiding in his work?

He couldn't bear the thought. She'd already shared with him her fears about the future and facing it alone. She certainly didn't need to go through this by herself. From now on, he wasn't going to hide from his feelings. He was going to tell her the truth as soon as he could.

No more regrets. Starting right now.

Gwen hated hospitals. It was a strange realization, given she worked in one. As a nurse, it was fine, but being a patient was the ultimate torture for any medical professional. Take your medicine. Eat your lime gelatin. Stay in bed. Listen to the medical advice of some twelve-year-old nurse who graduated from junior high while Gwen was graduating from nursing school.

Torture.

She would do whatever she had to do for Peanut's sake, but she wasn't going to be happy about it. Bed rest. Twelve to fourteen weeks of it. Absolute misery. She wanted to go home, and they promised she would be released soon, but that was little consolation. She would have enough short-term disability through work, but the reduced pay would barely cover her rent. And the doctor would not be pleased to know she lived alone in a fifth-floor walk-up she could barely afford.

That would mean either being lifted via crane into her apartment for the duration of her pregnancy or breaking down and staying with Adrienne and Will. Robert and Susan would help however they could, but they weren't in the financial position to pay her lost wages or put her up in a hotel. Their place was a slightly larger version of her own postage-stamp apartment. Letting go of her place and staying with Adrienne was the logical choice, as much as it pained her.

She hated this feeling of helplessness almost as much as she hated hospitals.

Gwen fought the urge to roll into a more comfortable position. The drugs had put a halt to the contractions, but they were taking every precaution. The doctor said it was best to lie on her left side, which was her least comfortable side, of course. It also put her back to the door of her room, so people were constantly sneaking up on her. At the very least, she wished her door would creak so she would know when someone was coming in.

"Gwen?"

At the sound of her name, Gwen jumped. Once again, someone had come in and startled her. After the sudden panic faded, a new fear crept into her mind. That voice. A man's voice.

Alex's voice.

Gwen leaned back to look over her shoulder. Alex was standing a few feet away from the bed, a small bundle of daisies in his hand. Knowing Alex, she'd figured he would show up with the largest, most expensive arrangement the hospital gift shop had to offer. The daisies were a charming, and unexpected, touch.

The doctor told her to try to avoid stressful situations, but what could she do when one walked into her hospital room? She wanted to roll back over and pretend he wasn't there, but that wasn't going to make it less stressful. Instead, she sat up and hit the button to bring the back of her bed up to a seated position. She fidgeted with smoothing out her hair and straightening her gown, but it was a lost cause.

She didn't say anything to him at first. She couldn't quite find the right words. First, there was a part of her that was embarrassed for running out without telling him goodbye. It was the coward's way out, but she never claimed to be brave when it came to relationships. Then there was the part of her pride that was wounded when he hadn't chased after her. She hadn't run with the intent of being chased, but it certainly would've been nice to know he cared enough to follow her.

There'd been no word from him since the holiday, but now he was showing up out of the blue with flowers. It made her wonder if she ever would've seen him again if she wasn't in the hospital. If not, she shouldn't read too much into his being here.

Gwen glanced down, uncomfortably, and noticed his

brown leather loafers were caked in dried mud and dirt. "Where on earth have you been?"

"New Orleans. I went to check on my high-rise, but I was coming back to see you when Adrienne called me."

A likely story. She wanted to believe that his being here had nothing to do with her condition, but it was doubtful. Adrienne had likely asked him to come, hoping it would make her feel better to see him. "There's no need to rush back here. I'm fine. Peanut is fine. We've just got to take it easy for a few months."

Alex nodded, his face unusually somber. "These are for you." He took a few steps forward to place the daisies on the table by her bed.

Gwen admired them for a moment. There were no roses or expensive lilies this time. Just a fresh bundle of white daisies with bright yellow centers. Despite her reluctance to accept his gift, they made her smile. They were her favorite flower, although there was no way he could know that. They grew wild on her grandparents' farm when she was a child. She would pick handfuls of them and her grandma would put them in a vase on the kitchen table.

"Thank you for the flowers."

Alex stood a few feet away, his posture unusually awkward. He appeared to be at quite a loss as to what to do with himself, which was odd for a man who was always in control of everything. "When Adrienne called, she mentioned you would have to take some time off work. I, uh, was thinking you might need someplace to stay for a few months. You know that my place has more than enough room. I'd have someone come in to cook for you. You wouldn't have to worry about bills or stairs or anything until the baby arrived safely."

Gwen's gaze narrowed at him. Part of her had hoped

he was here to make some romantic gesture, but she never once believed he was actually here to offer that same old song and dance again. "Did Adrienne ask you to do this?"

His gold eyes widened at the sudden venom in her voice. "What? No. She just told me you were on bed rest. I thought that—"

"You thought what, Alex? That you could just waltz in here like my knight in shining armor and I would be grateful for any scraps you threw my way? Don't you think next week's fling will wonder why there's a grumpy pregnant woman hiding away in your apartment like Mr. Rochester's crazy wife in *Jane Eyre*?"

He swallowed hard before he spoke. "That's not at all what I was thinking. I was just offering what I could to make your situation less stressful. I'm certain I've already caused you enough stress as it is. I'm sorry that you felt you had no other choice but to leave. I tried to call you over a dozen times after you left."

Gwen couldn't take her cell phone with her to work, but she was good about checking for voice mail or missed calls. "I didn't get any messages from you."

"That's because I never hit Send. I worried that you were right. That leaving was the best thing for you. I didn't want to drag you back into it if you wanted so desperately to be rid of me. So I decided to go to New Orleans and focus on work and let you get over me, if that's what you wanted."

Gwen only wished he was that easy to get over. The reality had been much tougher, even though she had been the one to leave. "But you said you were coming to see me, even before Adrienne called."

"Yes." He cleared his throat. "I was coming to tell you that I…"

Alex hesitated and she watched a touch of color drain from his face. His pupils were fully dilated, a touch of moisture breaking out across his brow.

"Are you about to pass out?" she asked. "Do I need to hit the call button for the nurse? I can't get up to catch you if you—"

"I love you, Gwen." Alex spit the words out as quickly as he could. It almost made her wonder if she'd heard him wrong. He could just as easily have said, "I loathe blue gin," although that would have been random and out of context.

"What did you say?" she asked. If he'd said what she thought he'd said, she wanted to hear it again. Louder and slower. Even if it made him squirm. Especially if it did.

Alex walked over to the bed and eased down beside her. He gently scooped up her hand, careful not to disturb her IV, and held it. "I...love you. You took my heart with you when you left, and I've had nothing but an aching hole in my chest these last few weeks. I'm stupid and stubborn, and it took me way too long to figure all this out. But I want to spend the rest of my life with you. I want to get married and have children of our own. I want to wake up every morning with you in my arms."

She'd always worried that Alex was too smooth for his own good and she would never be able to tell when he really meant what he said. But there was no doubt in her mind that he spoke the absolute truth to her now. There was a painful sincerity in the tone of his voice with no hint of his usual charming mischievousness. Alex was serious. And Gwen was dumbstruck. She couldn't even form the words that she loved him, too. All she could do was reach out to brush his honey-colored hair from his eyes. She let her hand linger on his cheek, his eyes closing as he leaned into her touch.

"When Adrienne called and said you were in the hospital with complications, there was this horrible moment where I thought I might've lost you forever. Or that something had happened to Peanut. I know she's not our child, but she's as close as I've ever come, and it would hurt just as badly to lose her. And to watch you go through that, knowing there was nothing I could do to help, would've broken my heart."

"I was so scared, Alex."

He leaned in to hug her, and the tears she'd been holding back since she was admitted to the hospital came rushing all at once. At first, she'd been too concerned to waste time crying, and then she hadn't had more than a few moments alone, with Adrienne, Robert and Susan hovering over her. Now, in Alex's arms, the dam broke.

"All I could keep thinking was that I'd messed up. And how crushed Robert and Susan would be if something happened to their little girl. I'd tried to do everything right. I just had one job—to keep their baby safe—and somehow, I'd failed."

"You didn't do anything wrong, Gwen," he whispered into her hair before sitting back to look her in the eye. "Sometimes these things happen. You're lucky you work at a hospital and had people around you who could help. It could've been so much worse. But everything is fine now. You and Peanut are safe. The doctors are going to keep a close eye on you. And like it or not, you're coming to live with me at least until she's born, if not for the rest of your life."

Gwen pulled back, the irritation on her face poorly disguised. "Now, what makes you think that telling me you love me gives you any more right to boss me around than before?"

"You're right," he conceded. "You're a grown woman who makes her own decisions. But I would very much like you to come stay with me. My apartment has felt cold and lonely since I got home. The memories of the weeks we'd spent there together were like ghosts, haunting me. I'd like us to make some new memories there. Unless you'd rather stay with Will and Adrienne...." He smiled.

At that, Gwen knew her argument was lost. It was one thing to be forced into staying with someone because they felt you couldn't take care of yourself. It was another entirely when they loved you and wanted to keep you safe and healthy. And she wanted to be with Alex. Just not as a burden. Her soft groan of defeat was enough encouragement for him.

"You're going to have the most comfortable and luxurious bed rest any pregnant woman has ever had. I'm not taking any chances with your health and welfare. The whole flight back here, I worried that I'd almost lost my chance. That because I was afraid to chase after you, you might never know how much I loved you."

"I knew," she whispered, a small smile curling her lips. "I was just waiting for you to get with the program."

Alex returned her smile. "I wish you would've told me that and saved me the last few weeks of angst."

"You wouldn't have listened. You needed to figure it out for yourself."

He nodded. "You're probably right. Does this mean that you'll agree to come stay at my place until the baby is born and possibly never move out?"

"Yes. I don't care if I ever see my miserable little apartment again."

"And you forgive me for letting a woman as great as you almost slip through my fingers?"

"Yes."

"And does it mean that you still love me, too? A little birdie told me that you did, but I want to hear it from the source."

"Yes. I do love you."

His hazel gaze searched her face for a moment, absorbing her answer before he spoke again. "Then I have one last question. And I hope that the answer to it will be yes, as well."

Gwen's breath caught in her throat. Just a minute earlier he'd mentioned marriage and children, but those were abstract plans for the future from a man who had just started wading into the commitment pool. If he was about to say what it sounded like he was going to say, some very concrete plans were about to be put in place.

Alex reached into his coat pocket and pulled out a small red box. "Will you, Miss Gwen Wright, do me the honor of being my wife?"

The top opened to a most unexpected find. The ring had a large yellow stone, surrounded by tiny diamonds and set into an intricate two-tone band with more tiny diamonds inset. It was beautiful. And unique. It had an antique feel about it, which made her think it was probably very old. Maybe a family heirloom. She would've been happy with any ring he gave her, but she appreciated him making the effort to give her something different.

Gwen knew in that moment that he really did love her and had for even longer than he knew. He'd paid attention to her, noticed the details, knew what she liked, put

her needs first, bought her things to make her happy...
It had just taken him this long to realize all those things
were the actions of a man in love.

Tears filled her eyes again, but at last, they were
happy tears. He wanted to marry her. Alex Stanton—
the man who made her laugh, made her smile, made her
feel like the sexiest woman on earth—was going to settle down with her. A nobody from Tennessee who had
wondered, not two days earlier, if she might be lonely
her whole life. "Yes."

Alex grinned wide and leaned in to gently embrace
her again. Gwen closed her eyes and relished the feel
of being in his arms—the warm scent of his skin and
cologne mingling, the heat of his body scalding her
through the thin cotton of her hospital gown. When he
pulled away, it was only to slip the ring on her finger
and kiss her properly.

On her long, lonely bus ride back to the city, Gwen
had searched her mind for their last kiss. It had been
nothing but a quick peck before they'd fallen asleep
in his room. It pained her to know that might be the
last kiss she ever shared with Alex. Now, with his lips
against hers and their futures intertwined, she no longer needed to worry. They would have many kisses to
fill her memory for years to come.

She never wanted to let him out of her arms' reach
again. And soon, she wouldn't have to.

"Now, I hate to go, but there's so much for me to
do before you're discharged. I'm going to go back to
my place and get it ready for you. If you give me your
keys, I'll have movers boxing up everything you own
before the end of the day. I'll handle everything, including talking to your landlord. I also have to make a very

important trip to my insurance agent to get that ring properly protected."

Gwen looked down at her engagement ring in a moment of confusion. It was beautiful, but was an insurance policy really necessary? Then it hit her. She examined it more closely and shook her head. "I suppose this isn't a really nice golden topaz, is it?"

Alex grinned and shook his head. "Would it make you feel better if I told you it was?"

Gwen shook her head and gazed at her ring again in amazement. A giant canary diamond. So typically Alex.

"Before I go, is there anything else I can do for you?"

"Loving me is enough." She smiled, then Peanut kicked at her. Gwen felt the relief wash over her, feeling the baby move again after the last twenty-four hours. Everything was going to be okay. She knew it now.

"But, if you don't mind smuggling in a hot fudge sundae…"

Epilogue

"I'm really starting to hate this car."

Alex frowned as he reached down to help Gwen out of the convertible. She was no longer pregnant, but only a couple weeks out from delivery, she was still too sore to climb out of the low bucket seats of his Corvette without help.

"We're getting married and having children. I am throwing away my little black book and putting my salacious ways behind me. But I draw the line at getting rid of this car. I will buy you a more sensible car of your own, if you insist."

Gwen eased up and planted a kiss on his pouty mouth. "I would never ask you to get rid of your baby. Maybe we could just put some monster truck wheels on it." She patted his shoulder playfully and the light sparkled off her engagement ring. The yellow oval diamond was dazzling in its antique setting, hit by the sunlight as it peeked through the bare branches and falling autumn leaves.

Alex took her hand and led her to the fellowship hall of the Trinity Wall Street Episcopal Church, where they were holding the belated baby shower. "I feel like I should've brought a gift," Gwen said, as they slipped through the heavy oak doors.

"I think you brought the baby, honey."

Gwen laughed and shook her head. "I still should've picked up something."

The hall was decorated in white and pink for a combined welcome celebration and baby shower. When Gwen was hospitalized, Robert and Susan had decided to hold out on having a shower. Now that Abigail was a healthy, happy, fifteen-day-old girl, party time had arrived.

The hall was filled with round tables, each alternating with pink or white tablecloths and centerpieces with bottles or candles. A spread of catered food lined one long table and ended in an adorable three-tiered diaper cake that had "Welcome Abby" in alphabet blocks along the bottom. Beside it was a large sheet cake with "Congratulations!" written on it in pink icing.

"Gwen!" Susan shouted from across the hall.

The crowd of people milling around all stopped to look in her direction. She had no doubt that they all knew who she was. Susan had been touting her as some sort of sacred vessel to anyone who would listen. It made Gwen a little uncomfortable, but one look into Susan's excited face melted it all away.

Susan came through the crowd with a white bundle in her arms. Abby was dressed in a pale pink and lace gown that had been in Susan's family for generations. Through the last few weeks of Gwen's bed rest, Susan had spent a lot of time with her. They'd chatted for hours about her plans for the nursery, her excitement about motherhood and details of Gwen's upcoming wedding. One day, Susan had brought the gown with her so Gwen could see it.

Gwen gently reached across the baby to hug Susan and smiled down at the tiny ivory-and-pink face of the most beautiful baby girl in the world. Despite the excitement, she was out cold in her mother's arms.

"Would you like to hold her? I feel bad that you haven't gotten to see her since you were discharged."

"Susan, she's your baby, not mine. You don't have to share custody with me."

Gwen stroked her finger along Abby's fat little cheek and whispered, "Hello, my Peanut." The baby stirred slightly at the sound of her voice, smiling sweetly in her sleep.

"What about you, Alex? You can get a little practice in for all those babies you'll be having soon."

Alex's eyes grew wide with panic, but before he could argue, the tiny infant was thrust into his uncertain arms. Gwen watched with amusement as he looked down at the baby as if she might sprout another head or start leaking something on him. But then, after a few moments, his expression softened and he watched Abby with a sense of newfound wonder.

Gwen felt the tiny prickle of tears as he gently swayed with her and hoped that one day soon, she would see him holding their own child just like this. "You're a natural."

"I've got a surprise for you," Susan said, pulling her away from the touching sight.

"For me? Why?"

"Robert and I talked about it, and we thought this would be a wonderful way to say thank-you."

Robert came over to them with a copy of the freshly issued birth certificate in his hands. After the adoption was finalized, it had to be redone with Susan's name as the legal mother. Gwen looked at it and was surprised to find the name *Abigail Gwendolyn Thatcher* written there.

"I thought you were naming her Abigail Rose?"

"We were, but we thought naming her after you would make it more meaningful. We always want Abby to know how special she is and how a wonderful person sacrificed so much to give her to us."

Now the tears were rolling in earnest. Gwen embraced Susan and then gave a hug to the reluctant Robert.

"They're crying again," he said to Alex. Apparently he had gotten his fill of crying women at the hospital the day Abby was born.

Alex shrugged. "They do that. As the father to a daughter, I suggest you get prepared. Here," he said, holding out Abby. "Hand one of them the baby. That will distract them."

Robert gave Abby over to Susan, who immediately stopped crying and started smiling again at the sight of her little girl.

Alex came up beside Gwen and wrapped his arm around her waist. "I never knew your name was Gwendolyn," he admitted.

"That's okay," she said with a smile as she stood on her toes to give him a kiss. "We've got our whole lives to learn everything we need to know about each other."

Alex gave her a sly grin and bent down to kiss her again. "I'm looking forward to every minute of it."

* * * * *

Harlequin® *Blaze*™

red-hot reads

He was looking for adventure…and he found her.

Kate Hoffmann

brings you another scorching tale

With just a bus ticket and $100 in his pocket, Dermot Quinn
sets out to experience life as his Irish immigrant grandfather
had—penniless, unemployed and living in the moment.
So when he takes a job as a farmhand, Dermot expects he'll
work for a while, then be on his way. The last thing he expects
is to find passion with country girl Rachel Howe, and his
wanderlust turning into a lust of another kind.

THE MIGHTY QUINNS: DERMOT

Available August 2012 wherever books are sold!